I0713001

COSCOM
ENTERTAINMENT

Praise for A.P. Fuchs's *Axiom-man*™

"Axiom-man is that unique breed of superhero that seems almost lost amid today's gaggle of the dark and tormented. He's nice, he cares, and his strength comes not from his fantastic powers, but from his soul. A.P. Fuchs has written a defining superhero novel."
    - Frank Dirscherl, author/creator of *The Wraith*

"*The Axiom-man Saga* has definitely won me over and I'm eagerly awaiting more adventures from the man in blue."
    - Stephen J. Semones, Director/Co-writer of
    The Wraith: Eyes of Judgment

"Reading *Axiom-man* is refreshing, like reading about the early days of Peter Parker, but with a cooler villain as well."
    - Jon Klement, author/creator of *Rush and the Grey Fox*

"Axiom-Man delivers all the things you loved about Silver and Bronze Age comics, but with the exciting edge and insightful prose you've come to expect of today's top writers! I highly recommend this book and series!"
    - Scott Story, *Johnny Saturn* artist and co-writer.

"*Axiom-man* was well worth reading and recommending. The broad appeal is amazing—from youth to adult, guys and girls. Superheroes might just become my thing."
    - Susan Kirkland, reviewer, *Calhoun Times*

"Fuchs brings to life a wonderfully imaginative hero we can all relate to . . . . If you're looking for something different, something truly creative, yet filled with action, look no further. *Axiom-man* is the end of your search."
— David Brollier, author of *The 3rd Covenant*

"I found myself picking the book up at various points in the day, just to read a little more."
— Darryl Sloan, author of *Ulterior* and *Chion*

"If you're an action fan with moral sensibilities you'll not just enjoy *Axiom-man*, you'll wish you were he."
— Frank Creed, author of *Flashpoint*

"Plenty of surprising twists and turns in this highly enjoyable story. It'll leave you wanting more. Axiom-man is a delightfully human superhero with true depth and spirituality."
— Grace Bridges, author of *Faith Awakened*

"Fuchs's writing style is immediately likable, light and airy, with a touch of wholesomeness that renders Axiom-man appropriate for kids and adults alike. I anxiously await the further adventures of Axiom-man. Highly recommended."
— Gina Ranalli, author of *13 Thorns*

"If you dig superhero tales that are loaded with action and fun, look no further."
— Nick Cato, *Horror Fiction Review*

"A must read that I cannot recommend enough."
— Joe Kroeger, *Horror World*

ALSO BY A.P. FUCHS

Undead World Trilogy

Blood of the Dead

THE AXIOM-MAN™ SAGA
(listed in reading order)

Axiom-man
Episode No. 0: First Night Out
Doorway of Darkness
Episode No. 1: The Dead Land
City of Ruin
Of Magic and Men (comic book)

FICTION

A Stranger Dead
A Red Dark Night
April (writing as Peter Fox)
Magic Man (deluxe chapbook)
The Way of the Fog (The Ark of Light Vol. 1)
Devil's Playground (written with Keith Gouveia)
On Hell's Wings (written with Keith Gouveia)

NON-FICTION

Book Marketing
for the Financially-challenged Author

POETRY

The Hand I've Been Dealt
Haunted Melodies and Other Dark Poems
Still About A Girl

www.apfuchs.com
&
www.undeadworldtrilogy.com

AXIOM-MAN™
THE DEAD LAND

by

A.P. FUCHS

COSCOM ENTERTAINMENT
WINNIPEG

Coscom Entertainment
130 Stanier Street
Winnipeg, MB R2L 1N3 Canada

ISBN 978-1-897217-83-2

Published by Coscom Entertainment
www.coscomentertainment.com
Text set in Garamond
Printed and bound in the USA
Cover art by Justin Shauf and Kyle Zajac
Edited by Ryan C. Thomas
Interior author photo by Roxanne Fuchs

Library and Archives Canada Cataloguing in Publication

Fuchs, A. P. (Adam Peter), 1980-
    Axiom-man : the dead land / A.P. Fuchs.

"Episode #1"
ISBN 978-1-897217-83-2

    I. Title.

PS8611.U34A942 2008   C813'.6   C2008-903742-1

For Justin Shauf, who is not only an amazing artist,
but also a fantastic friend.

AXIOM-MAN™

THE DEAD LAND

PROLOGUE

FOR THE FOURTH time that night Payton Marsch heard the muffled low and raspy groan coming from his closet.

He checked the clock: 1:48 A.M. Three minutes since the last groan. The previous one had occurred after a six-minute silence. The other two he hadn't bothered to time, but he did know that they were spaced further apart.

Buried in his sheets, the comforter so huge that it engulfed his seven-year-old frame, he rolled over onto his side, facing away from the closet door. Even at his young age he knew it was unwise to turn your back on potential danger, but at the same time he drew comfort from this small effort to make himself stronger.

His father would have wanted it that way.

"Big boys don't complain or cry out for their dads at the first sign of trouble," his father'd been telling him over the past six months.

He lay there, body curled up, knees drawn tight against his chest. The muscles in his back were weak and loose from the fear of what might be in his closet making that noise.

Eyes closed, he prayed that sleep would come and after a nice long dream, he'd open his eyes to the morning light that always spilled through the window just above the headboard. He'd walk to school with Dave, settle into class, and by first recess, tonight would be nothing but a faded memory.

I wish my door was open, he thought. His father was adamant about bedroom doors being shut at night. A fire hazard if they're left open, he'd say.

"Gotta be safe should something happen," Payton was told more than once.

Dad had never been the safety freak of the family, but ever since Mom didn't come home last month, Dad had changed. He was more paranoid, more unsure, and the man that Payton once thought of as his own personal Axiom-man was now just a mere mortal.

His eyes snapped open as the low, raspy groan seeped from behind the closet doors again. He cringed beneath his sheets, sucking his body up into an even tighter ball. Dare he look at the clock?

"No fear, no fear, no fear," he whispered and forced himself to roll over.

It was 1:49. Probably 1:49:30, if the red digital display on the little black clock showed seconds.

It's getting closer. Though he was just learning the art of telling time in school—something he had a little difficulty grasping, especially when dealing with those catalogue clocks—no wait, fire log clocks?—that wasn't it either, but whatever they were called, it didn't matter. Point was, he understood that there were sixty seconds in a minute, which was different than one hundred pennies in a dollar. And half a minute was thirty seconds, so that meant the next time he heard the sound, it would be less than a minute from now.

He closed his eyes and focused on the math. Though he was ahead of his class and already grasping the basic concepts of division, what he wouldn't give for a pencil and paper to make figuring this out easier. Less than a minute, less than a minute, less than . . .

Thirty-five seconds? Forty?

Wait. A minute and a half is ninety seconds, right? So half that is . . . um . . . half is . . . forty . . . forty-one, forty-two, forty-three, forty-four, yeah, forty-five seconds. Less than a minute. I was right!

That "less than a minute" quickly came round and once more another groan came from his closet, this time louder.

"Dad . . ." he whispered, half-expecting his father to hear him all the way to his bedroom at the end of the hall. "Dad, wake up. It's almost here. Dad."

Half of forty-five . . . His jaw dropped. *There is no half of forty-five. Five can't be split in half!*

"Oh no," he said louder than he meant to and quickly slapped a palm over his mouth to keep himself quiet.

He peeked over at the closet door. The white dual-doors joined together by a pair of hinges, which were gray in the darkness that covered his bedroom, sat there, unassuming, the wood the only thing separating himself from whatever was within.

Another groan.

A shockwave zipped up and down Payton's chest and his breathing kicked into overdrive.

"It's almost here," he mouthed, the only sound escaping his lips the sibilance of the letter S.

Hands shaking, he ducked under his quilt.

"Dad, come here. Dad, come here. Dad, come here."

His father never came.

He had to scream—*needed* to—and make some kind of noise to alert his father to what was going on. His closet had never made noise before. The clothes inside didn't make noise. Even the toys and board games lining the top shelf within were quiet ones.

Something was inside there.

"Gggrrruuuhhh . . ." The sound. That awful sound.

"Dad! DAD!"

The closet doors creaked open, their squeal against the hinges sending a wild tingle up and down Payton's arms. His body locked. He couldn't move.

"DAD!" He pictured himself throwing the comforter and sheet off his body, leaping out of bed, throwing open the bedroom door and bounding down the hall and barreling into his father's room to seek solace beside his dad's big and warm body. The mental image was so clear and so real that Payton's heart broke when he realized that he was still in bed, cowering beneath the sheets.

"Hhrrrgggrrrrhhhhhuuuuhhhh . . ."

"Dad!" His voice caught in his throat and when he tried to call out again, only a soft "Da" escaped his lips.

Silence.

Payton remained there in the dark beneath his quilt, hugging his knees to his chest, head pressed tightly against his kneecaps. "Go away, go away, go away." Breathing hard and breathing deep, he waited there in morbid apprehension. Any moment now, whatever was within his closet would come out, whip back his bed sheets and rip him to pieces.

Yet nothing happened.

The moments ticked by. One minute? Two? He didn't know. He didn't have a clock here under the covers to help him keep track of time.

"Big boys aren't afraid of the dark," his father told him last week when he took away his nightlight. "You're going to spend your whole life sleeping in a dark room. You'll be safe. There's nothing to be afraid of."

If only he could hear those words now: "There's nothing to be afraid of."

Dad, you just don't know. Dad, you're not here. You never hear me. Tears leaked out from the corners of his eyes.

"I wish you were here," Payton said, his voice heavy with grief.

Snot leaked from his nose; he wiped it against his knees, the snot's dampness seeping through his pajama pants to the skin beneath.

The moments ticked by.

Silence. The whole house was quiet.

His heart began to slow and his breathing calmed down.

"I think it's gone," he whispered. "H-hello?"

No reply.

More than anything he wanted to be strong. More than anything he wanted to show his father he was brave and that he could face the dark.

Be fast. You can do it. He gripped the comforter near his head. *One . . .* He squeezed the quilt even tighter. *Two . . .* Tighter still. *Just go fast.* And he prepared the word "Dad" to come screaming out of his lips should he need it. *Three!*

He threw the quilt forward, ripping it from over his head.

There was no one there. The room was quiet. The room was dark.

The closet door was open, offering a gateway to endless black.

A rush of heat coated Payton's skin and sweat burst from his pores.

He sat there for several minutes, his lips pursed, breathing out the fear.

The clock read 1:54.

Ears perked, he listened again for the groaning. Listened for any sign of life in the house.

Quiet. Absolute silence.

Heart beating quickly, he thought maybe that groaning was his imagination after all, that the closet—which needed to be closed all the way to remain shut thanks to its janky hinges—that maybe that groaning was just built up tension in the frame.

The thought brought a smile to his face and a sudden feeling of foolishness. Perhaps his dad was right. Perhaps he *was* a scaredy-cat.

"I thought . . ." he started. "Stupid."

He slowly swung his legs over the side of the bed, slid his bottom to the edge then planted his feet on the plush carpet. When he stood, it took a couple of steps for his feet to be sure beneath him, his legs still rubbery from the ordeal.

The closet loomed before him, its inside pitch black, an endless pit of the unknown.

Just close it then go to bed. Don't tell Dad tomorrow. His heart ached. *He'll just make you feel bad.*

"Just do it quick," he said quietly and stretched out his hand to push closed the dual-door.

Something stirred in the dark.

Before Payton could scream, a gray hand snapped out of the dark and grabbed him.

CHAPTER ONE

AXIOM-MAN TUCKED HIS head down when a gust of freezing wind whipped against his face.

"Man, I hate this," he muttered.

The cold wasn't so bad at street level or in between the buildings, but up here, above the ring of suburbia that surrounded the downtown area, it was downright unbearable at times.

Winter's right around the corner. Good thing there's no snow yet. Gonna have to come up with a good way to keep warm. Tights ain't gonna cut it once it hits minus forty-five.

This was the third night in a row where he spent a lot of time just flying around, not really on patrol—though he always helped out when the city streets lit up with red and blue sirens—and tried to clear his head. For a long time after Redsaw opened the Doorway of Darkness at the MTS Centre, things had been pretty much normal: go to work during the day, hit the streets at night, come home to the occasional message from Valerie Vaughan, then try and sleep and avoid the crazy notion of calling her back so late. Why she was calling him, he didn't know. It wasn't like her. But lately, images from that night at the MTS Centre filled his mind, that terrible red lightning-lined doorway sitting there on the stage, the putrid black smoke pouring out from it. Redsaw flying into the doorway. Chasing after him. The voice in that other world promising Redsaw rule over this one. The fight, the blood, the near-death experience.

He just needed to sort things out and flying around was the best remedy for that. The only problem was that his mind kept going back to Valerie and wondering why she was trying to contact him. So far as he knew, she thought he was a loser as Gabriel Garrison. Even their "date" at Oscar Owen's ball had been his helping her out because her original date had bailed on her at the last moment. He just wished he knew what she wanted and getting in touch with her throughout the day was impossible with Dolla-card's policy of not using their phones for personal calls. And he was already in hot water with them as it was due attendance problems in the past (though recently he had been showing up to work on time every day in an effort to put the past further and further behind him). Perhaps this weekend he'd finally get around to calling her back. That was, if he could do it without stumbling over his own tongue and breathing all short and heavy. Being branded as a nerd was bad enough; the last thing he needed was for her to think he was creepy, too. Why she got him into a knot, he didn't know. Just part of being in lo—

Tiny red and blue lights materialized below and the shrill sound of sirens wafted up into the air, snapping him from his thoughts.

Two cop cars, one riding the other's tail.

Wonder what's going on? He adjusted his flight path to match the direction the cars were going in.

They were over the west end. Something being wrong wasn't surprising. The west end was notorious for B and Es, hookers lining the corners and frequent stabbings.

Axiom-man got his head in the game and shoved aside any thoughts of his life as Gabriel Garrison, keeping himself focused on the task at hand. Gabriel's problems could wait.

Below, the squad cars stopped in front of a small house. The second the break lights flashed off, two officers quickly emerged from each vehicle. Axiom-man flew onto the property and touched down in between the two pairs of officers. The first pair was at the house's door and the other was running up the broken cement-padded walkway leading up to it.

The cops stopped in their tracks, one male and one female. Axiom-man recognized the female officer as Judy, the same cop who had been on the scene back when there had been trouble at the McGillary house in North Kildonan.

Judy's blue eyes lit up with warmth at his arrival. The male officer's just hit him with a cool gaze, the perfect picture of how the Winnipeg Police Service felt about him.

"Could have given us a warning you were coming," Judy said.

The two officers at the door, both male, peeked back over their shoulders. They, too, gave him an "Oh, it's him" kind of look before returning their attention to the door then rapping on it.

"It was last minute," Axiom-man said, folding his arms across his chest. "Besides, I don't have a way to contact you."

"You mean Gunn didn't get in touch with you yet?"

Jack Gunn, the name that brought both comfort and disdain to Axiom-man's mind. The guy was as tough-as-nails as you could get when it came to a cop. He was a sergeant last time Axiom-man checked, though that could have changed now—after the fiasco at the MTS Centre, he had been put in charge of a new super-powered task force designed specifically for events that brought out men in tights. As of late, that had only been Axiom-man. Redsaw had fallen off the radar. Hopefully it was permanent, though Axiom-man doubted it if that mysterious promise of rule to Redsaw was any indicator.

"No. Was he supposed to?"

"He's supposed to do a lot of things," the male cop said.

"And you are?"

"Manks." He didn't hold out his hand for a handshake.

The cops turned their attention to the door when it squeaked on its hinges and a man whose brown hair was riddled with male-pattern baldness appeared, his eyes wet with tears. Axiom-man couldn't see his whole face with the cops standing in front of him. He wore an ill-fitting white T-shirt and boxers.

The cops at the door said something to the man, but Axiom-man couldn't hear what; Manks's voice drowned it out. "Yeah, he's here," Manks said into the radio on his shoulder.

Judy mouthed the name "Gunn" to Axiom-man.

Axiom-man shook his head then stepped toward the door to get a better look at the man in his underwear that was ushering the cops into the old house. The man set his eyes on him and while trying to discern what the wide-eyed gaze meant, Axiom-man's heart skipped a beat when he saw whose house this was: old Tom's, one of the guys he worked with at Dolla-card. They weren't friends or even close coworkers. The most interaction they had was the occasional swapping of callback forms or asking to borrow a pen.

Axiom-man pretended he didn't know him and proceeded toward the three-step flight of stairs leading to a small cement pad at the foot of the door, but not before hearing Manks whisper to Judy, "He'll be here right away. Don't let the cape leave before he does."

Ignoring the twitch of anger that pinched his heart, Axiom-man thanked Tom for holding the door open for him. Tom just nodded and waited for Judy and Manks to step further into the house.

Muffled voices came from down the hall and Axiom-man followed their sound. The floor creaked with every step; the dated wooden framing on the doors and the smell of dust on the air screamed that this was an old home built in the early 1900s. The voices led him to a little boy's room, the light on. Just a lone light bulb, no shade.

The two male cops standing in the center of the room, talking with hands on hips, eyed him coolly when he stood under the doorframe.

The three stared each other down and not for the first time in his career as a crimefighter did Axiom-man wish he had a better rapport with Winnipeg's finest. Was he supposed to ask what was going on? A part of him thought that by now, after having been active in the city for the better part of a year, he wouldn't have to ask what happened, that it would be a given what he was doing at any crime scene.

One of the cops, the taller one with short, spiked black hair, said, "Missing person. Possibly a kidnapping."

"Maybe a runaway, though the window's not open," the other officer said, jutting a thumb in the direction of the window.

So it could be anything, Axiom-man thought. "How old?"

"Seven. A boy."

"When did the call come in?"

"About twenty minutes ago."

"So not long."

The cop with the spiked hair raised his eyebrows and snarked, "Yeah."

"But how long *really* has it been? An hour? Two? When did To—when did the boy's father know his son was missing?"

Tom's broken voice came up behind him and Axiomman cleared the way for the man to enter his son's room. His voice broke with nearly every syllable. "All I heard was the tail-end of him calling my name. I'm a heavy sleeper. Who knows how many times he called till I finally heard him?"

The two male cops leaned into each other. "You wanna . . . ?"

"Sure."

"And I'll . . . ?"

"Yeah."

The two left the room. Tom furrowed his brow.

A few seconds later, Judy and Manks took their place. Each eyed the room, taking in all its corners. It was a boy's room, no doubt about it, with a huge Transformers poster above the bed, the floor littered with toys of the same and a spilled-over, big blue bucket of LEGO.

The white closet door stood open, a few T-shirts and a pair of pants strewn along its floor, presumably from Tom rummaging around in there, thinking maybe his son was hiding inside. A small pile of laundry with no basket sat in its middle.

Down the hall, the front door creaked open and Jack Gunn's unmistakable voice filled the landing: "Is he still here?"

Great. Haven't even had a chance to start yet. I'm not taking any guff from that guy no matter what he says.

The other male cops, who were probably looking around the home, tried talking to Gunn. All Axiom-man heard was Gunn snap, "Yeah, yeah, yeah," then the grumpy cop's heavy footfalls as he overrode the creaking of the floor and made his way to the bedroom.

"You two, out," Gunn said, pointing at Judy and Manks.

Manks shot Axiom-man a "You got it coming" look, while Judy merely rolled her eyes.

Axiom-man moved out of the way and let the cops pass. *I'm going to have to get in touch with her sometime soon. I'm getting sick of being treated like dirt all the time.*

Gunn, still wearing his famous brown leather overcoat even though the thing could hardly keep him warm in this kind of weather, turned to Tom. "Please excuse us, Mr. Marsch. I know this is a trying time for you. If you wouldn't mind, would you please join Judy and Manks in the other room and tell them everything you can remember from tonight and if anything comes to mind that might have caused this tragedy: strange phone calls, possibly some tension between you and your son, people driving by the house or strangers showing up at the door, unwanted solicitors—anything that might provide a clue as to who or what might have caused this? I just want you to know, though, that we have put an APB out on your son."

Tom nodded; Gunn stroked his salt-and-pepper, short-trimmed beard, as if he could hardly wait for Tom to leave the room.

Jack put a hand on Tom's shoulder as the man turned and left the room. Axiom-man wished he could have said something, but he didn't know what.

Once Tom was gone, Gunn closed the bedroom door then turned to face Axiom-man.

"So, spill it," Gunn said, leaning against the wall with one hand, the other on his hip.

"Spill what?"

"You showed up here. This isn't your thing."

"And what *is* my thing, Gunn?"

Jack slid his hand off the wall. "You don't do missing persons."

Axiom-man wanted to say, "Neither do you," but didn't.

Gunn made an elaborate wave with his hand. "You swoop down, stop a bad guy and leave him for us. Where were you in this?"

"Didn't it occur to you that maybe I saw the sirens and came to see what the problem was? It wouldn't have been the first time, Jack. Listen, whatever your beef with me is, let it go, at least for now. You got a boy missing and a terrified father in the other room. You and I are standing in the middle of the crime scene. Wouldn't you think it prudent for you and me to look around and see if we could find any clues as to what happened here tonight?" *That should shut him up.*

Gunn took one giant step toward him and stood so close that his toes touched the tips of Axiom-man's boots. The stocky cop's breath stunk with stale coffee and one too many plates of leftover Chinese food.

Jack's bushy eyebrows furrowed and his brown-eyed gaze bore into him, his chin jutting out as if defying Axiom-man to take a shot at him.

"If you had anything to do with this, if I find out you *were* here and you somehow let the boy slip through your fingers, I swear that mask is coming off. And I'm going to make a spectacle about it. I don't care what you do for this city. You can't be trusted. You know it and I know it."

With a push from his fingers, Axiom-man shoved Gunn in the chest, forcing him to stumble back a few steps.

"Get off my boots," Axiom-man said.

Before Gunn could retaliate or say something smart, there was a knock at the door. Jack stared at Axiom-man for a solid twenty seconds before opening it. Judy was on the other side. "Phil from Missing Person's is here," she said.

Still eyeing Axiom-man, Jack said, "Tell him I'll be right there." Turning to her, "And get Manks in here. Don't want this guy in here alone. Sweep the room."

She nodded, glanced Axiom-man's way, her gaze asking what just happened between the two.

Judy went down the hall.

"He's coming," she told someone in the other room.

"Tell him to hurry. This isn't his thing."

"But Axiom-man—"

"Axiom-man can stay there." Louder: "Gunn!"

Gunn stayed and stared a moment longer before turning to follow her. Finally, he left.

Jerk, Axiom man thought.

He looked around the room. He wasn't a detective nor did he have any formal training in police work. The most he knew about what to do came from a handful of Google searches on crime scene investigation, but even those turned up scant information about what to do specifically. The best move, he figured, was to first look for signs of a struggle.

None. No real mess to indicate a little boy thrashing about as someone grabbed him.

His eyes drifted over to the closet and the bunched up T-shirt and jeans on the floor and the pile of laundry at its center.

He took a step closer to the closet.

The smell hit him.

He'd recognize it anywhere.

"It can't be," he whispered and crouched down by the clothes on the floor. The stink was unmistakable, that awful stench of rotten fish mixed with week-old garbage, the same smell that poured out of the Doorway of Darkness along with that black smoke.

Axiom-man poked at the laundry on the floor. The bottoms of the white socks were stained brown, one of the red T-shirts had a grass stain, bringing to mind Christmas holly.

Judy and Manks came in.

"Find anything?" Judy asked.

"Is he even supposed to be—"

"Shh." To Axiom-man: "Find anything?"

Axiom-man eyed the laundry pile. "No. Nothing that I could—" What was that? A thin trail of slick browny-green goop snaked along the floor, gathered in patches in places, as thin as hairs in others. He dabbed at it with his gloved finger then brought it a few inches from his nose. He knew this smell, too: human waste. But there was something else mixed in with it, as well, but he couldn't quite place it.

He smeared his finger on one of the socks, wiping it off, then turned his attention toward the back of the closet.

Once more he was greeted by the foul stench of rotten fish. This couldn't be. The Doorway of Darkness had been sealed. The doorway hadn't even been in this room.

He parted back the clothing to get a better look at the source of the smell. Judy came down beside him and leaned over his shoulder.

"What did you find?" she asked.

It was a moment before he answered. The dark of the back of the closet didn't provide much detail. "You better back up."

"Why?"

"Just do it."

"Jack?" Manks called out the door.

Jack didn't reply so Manks got on his radio.

"Oh, that stinks," Judy said and covered her nose and mouth.

"Stand aside," Axiom-man said, and stood.

Judy did the same and took a step back.

Manks called for Jack with the radio.

Axiom-man tore the boy's clothes off the clothes rack and threw them to the side just outside the closet door.

Lining the inside wall adjacent to the rear of the closet was a thin film of charcoal-black smoke. It danced along the wall like dry ice.

"What is that?" Judy asked.

Axiom-man put a hand against her, keeping her from coming any closer. "Please, stay there."

Jack's stomping footfalls neared the room.

Axiom-man took a step closer toward the film of black smoke. He powered up his eyes and shot a quick blast of blue energy against it, preparing himself for it to suddenly come alive and attack him. Instead, the energy beam zipped into the black and was swallowed whole.

I've seen you before. I'm not afraid, he thought to himself. Of all days, he hadn't expected today to be the day he'd again face the Doorway of Darkness.

Slowly, he reached out his hand toward the murk.

Jack Gunn entered the room.

Axiom-man's fingers grazed the smoke. An electric tingle shot through his hands. Powering up his eyes, he got himself ready for whatever he might face.

The film of black smoke danced along his hand like faeries prancing in the wind.

Then it latched onto him and sucked him in.

CHAPTER TWO

BLACK SMOKE SURROUNDED him, blocking out any source of light. Axiom-man couldn't move, couldn't breathe, couldn't do anything but let his body be taken by the dark. The black smoke violently tossed him side to side, front and back, and before his heart could even jump into panic mode, the smoke gave him one violent push and coughed him out . . . back into the closet.

Axiom-man stumbled against the interior wall, tripped over his own feet, then landed on his behind, his eyes fixed on the film of black smoke lining the interior side wall of the closet. The smoke lingered there a moment then faded away.

"Gunn?" he said. No answer.

Upon further inspection he saw someone had turned off the lights to the room. The only illumination was a weird gray light coming in through the window. That smell returned, the funk of waste matter mixed with rotten fish. The greeny-brown slop was smeared on the floor around him. Axiom-man shot to his feet to avoid sitting in it. None seemed to have gotten on his uniform though he couldn't be completely sure.

A trail of the green-brown mess led out of the closet. Axiom-man followed it. The bedroom door was open; the hallway beyond was dark. No voices. No footfalls. No creaking of the floorboards.

The house was empty.

"Hello?" he called. Nothing.

He ran out of the room, down the hall and to the front landing. "Hey, Jack!"

No reply.

What's going on? When the black smoke first grabbed hold of him, he expected to be drawn into that strange world of nothing but red and black clouds and blasts of red lightning that seemed to have it in for him. Whatever just happened, it wasn't the Doorway of Darkness. This was something entirely different.

Axiom-man opened the front door and stepped out onto the cement pad outside. The sky was overcast with deep gray clouds, coffee-brown streaks running through them, no breeze on the air. It wasn't cold, like it had been earlier that night. Instead, a coolness akin to fall hung on the air. No wind. No sounds. The branches of the trees lining the street were bare, the bark cracked and gray, as if they hadn't received a good rain in a long, long time.

All the houses seemed void of life. A few cars parked on the street were without drivers, many coated in what appeared to be dried gray paint, as if the sky itself had dumped a bucket of the stuff on them. The ground, too.

"Where am I?" he said quietly.

The trail of green-brown gunk continued down the steps then faded out down the cement pads leading up to the door. More than likely whatever caused this foul path of goop was what took Tom's kid. Axiom-man didn't even know the boy's name. There hadn't been time to ask. His heart ached at having not been more attentive to such a crucial detail. A name was everything sometimes.

Should he stay put? Should he look around?

He went back inside and quickly made his way back to the boy's bedroom. Back into the closet. No film of black cloud along the interior wall. He had hoped the thing would have reappeared and he'd take his chances entering it again. It might have led him home.

"I'm trapped," he said and leaned a hand against the wall. His eyes ached and a subtle headache formed at the top of his head. The watch beneath his glove told him it was near 3 A.M. The only thing that stopped the headache from getting any worse was the adrenaline pounding through his system.

Axiom-man went back outside and once again stood on the front steps. He had hoped that maybe someone might be coming down one of the sidewalks or someone might be moving around in one of the windows of the houses across the street. Instead, the windows were dark and the sidewalks were empty of all life.

Not knowing what else to do, he balled up his fists and tore off into the sky, getting as high and as far away from the empty street as possible.

He needed answers.

———

Every city street was the same: empty with not a soul in sight. The streets were clogged with vehicles; every time Axiom-man swooped down to see if someone was inside one of them, he was greeted by empty seats and opened doors, as if the driver had run out in a mad panic. None of the houses or windows of the apartment buildings had their lights on, each window a block of shadow against brick that was washed over in that sickly gray paint. It wasn't until he got to the thick of downtown that he paused in the air, the weight of isolation finally getting to him.

This isn't the Winnipeg I know.

Below, amidst the cars parked at odd angles, the turned-over garbage cans, the broken windows and dried gray puddles that patched the landscape, military vehicles dotted the pavement. A dark green Jeep was up on one of the curbs, another had its front end bashed in against a streetlamp. Two seemed to be locked together from a head-on collision. An overturned tank sat near the Hudson Bay Company.

A cop car sat half in-half out of the Staples at the corner of Portage Place. A fire truck was up on the sidewalk one street over, its ladder partly extended as if the original goal had been to reach the roof.

To get away from something.

Axiom-man scanned the streets again for any sign of life. He even went so far as searching the skies above the city, hoping to see a plane or helicopter—somebody he could flag down and talk to and figure out what was going on. He even scanned the horizon looking for Redsaw, the only other man on the face of the earth who could fly. Despite the fact Redsaw was dangerous and any encounter with him would inevitably lead to a fight, right now it didn't matter.

He couldn't be alone.

Taking deep breaths, trying to calm his speeding heart, Axiom-man slowly sank to street level.

He cupped his hands around his mouth. "Hello!" *Please let there be someone. Please let there be someone.* "Hello!"

Nothing. The air was quiet. Dead quiet. Not even a breeze.

"Is everyone indoors or . . ."

He floated upward and got above the rooftops.

"I can't be the only one here," he said. "There's no way the entire city, perhaps even the planet, is empty. I know it's the middle of the night, but still. Someone—at least *a* person—should be up."

If anybody was around, if indeed all were hiding, and if someone saw him through one of the windows, they would surely flag him down.

For an hour he searched the city, dipping in between the buildings, flying in between the cars, past houses and under bridges—anywhere that a person might be near.

Still nothing.

He set down beside an old orange and yellow transit and walked around the bus, checking it over. No one was inside. When he rounded the rear of the vehicle, he stopped and felt his mouth slacken beneath his mask. The rear window was caked with dark red, dry and smeared. A bloody handprint marked the corner of the window. The cars around it, some up on curbs, others spun around facing the wrong way on the road, all carried a similar dark red. He didn't need anyone to tell him what it was.

Blood.

He walked between the cars. Some had bloody streaks across their hoods. Others had handprints on the windows or dark red rimming the wheel wells. A few had blacky-red streaks across the doors, as if someone with a gushing wound had been scraped across them.

Did all the cars have this? He couldn't remember. So lost in the confusion of panic, searching for any sign of life, he hadn't paid attention to what the cars looked like. Just noted they were empty and moved on.

Was I that scared? He would have thought that after all he'd witnessed since gaining his powers, since all he'd been through, since all the weird creatures and haunting voices, he would have been sharper, more attuned to his surroundings.

But death was always new, no matter when it happened or who it happened to. Yet . . .

He stopped walking when a single thought took him: had death and blood become so commonplace in his life that they had become part of the everyday?

"I couldn't have become that numb so quickly," he whispered.

Perhaps he had turned a corner. Perhaps this is what happened to all who gave their lives in service to others. Those like him—cops, firemen, emergency workers, soldiers—all who were regularly exposed to the other side of life: death. They saw things regular people didn't see, heard things people weren't supposed to hear, were part of things that your average person had no idea existed.

He and others like him were part of a world of evil. The part of life that folks admitted existed but never understood.

"There's gotta be somebody here," he said. He glanced up toward the city's skyline. "Valerie."

Axiom-man kicked off from the ground and sped toward her place.

———

Valerie Vaughan's apartment was not far from the heart of the city. Axiom-man had only been there a few times but her address was something he couldn't forget. You always remembered where those you loved lived.

He had to see her. She was the only one he could talk to, the only one he connected with while in the cape. Whatever was going on between her and him as Gabriel, that didn't matter. She still thought Gabriel and Axiom-man were two separate people and treated them as such.

And it was only as Axiom-man that he could talk to her, *really* talk to her.

Once over her building, he floated down to her fourth-floor balcony and touched down. There wasn't any gray paint, only a thin film of the stuff on the railing, the floor above her suite having protected it from whatever had fallen from the sky however long ago.

Valerie's balcony window was dark, the lights inside turned off or no longer working.

Axiom-man tapped on the glass, hoping that she was there and just in another room. *Please be here. Please be here.*

She didn't come.

He tapped on the glass, this time harder.

"Come on."

No answer.

"Valerie!"

The glass shattered as his knuckles broke through, the pieces falling in front of his boots like rain. He didn't mean to hit the glass so hard. Just couldn't help it.

"Oh great," he whispered and stepped into her apartment.

All was cast in shadow.

"Valerie?" He listened for footsteps or any sign of life from the other rooms.

The couch to the side had a few pillows on it, propped up against one of the armrests as if someone had been napping, but by the look of the cushions, no one had sat there in a long time. A picture of Valerie and her family was on a small table next to a chair near the couch, a snapshot from a time before the sky went gray and all was abandoned.

Axiom-man found a light switch near the kitchen. He clicked it up and down. It didn't work.

The kitchen was empty; a few dirty dishes were in the sink, the smell of old food sharp on the air. He could only imagine what the fridge smelled like.

"Val?" he said.

The bathroom was empty, the shower curtain partly drawn, gray sweatpants hanging over the curtain rod. He knew those sweatpants. They were the same ones she wore that day he interrupted her jog by the Legislative Building and first took her flying.

Axiom-man cautiously made his way to the bedroom, each step deliberate and painful, the sharp image of her limp body lying on the bed, dead, invading his mind and staying there no matter how many times he tried to push it out.

"Val?" he said softly. His voice pinched at the back of his throat. Tears dampened the corners of his eyes beneath his mask. "Please be alive. Only sleeping."

The bedroom door was closed but not locked in the catch. He placed a palm against it and prepared himself for the worst. The door creaked when he slowly swung it open.

Empty.

The scent of dust hung on the air. No one had been here in a long time. The bed was half-made, the dresser drawers open with a few clothes and undergarments hanging out, as if she had packed and left in a hurry. The closet door was open, too. Axiom-man went over to it and tried the light switch next to it. No power. Work blouses and evening dresses hung symmetrically along the rack. Shirts and pants a few inches over hung in disarray on the plastic hangers. A couple hangers were on the floor.

"I really needed you to be here," he said quietly.

He went and examined the clothes, subconsciously looking for a clue as to where she went though he knew full well they wouldn't tell him anything in regards to her whereabouts.

He just needed to "see her," to be around the outfits she wore when she worked with him at Dolla-card.

He touched one of the sleeves of a white blouse he liked seeing her in. His eyes trailed over to the black dress she wore the night of Oscar Owen's ball. He could almost see her in it, the way it fit her perfectly, accenting every right curve, hiding others. Her gorgeous brown eyes and rich brown hair beautiful that night, just like every day he got to see her at work. But no longer. She didn't work with him anymore and he hadn't seen her as Axiom-man since the night Redsaw opened the Doorway of Darkness.

The doorway.

His mind immediately focused on it, the red lines framing the entrance to another world. The black smoke pouring out of it; the realm of endless red and black cloud beyond.

That voice.

He needed the messenger. If anyone had answers, it would be the one who gave him his powers. But the only way to contact the messenger was via his computer, and if Valerie's apartment and the rest of the city was any indicator, the power was out all over. Should he go home? Was there anything left of it?

"I don't know," he said, walking out of the bedroom.

Stepping into the gray light coming in from the broken balcony window was a fresh reminder of the world he had come into. In the dark of the bedroom, it somehow had seemed more distant, even forgotten for a few moments. Out here . . .

The world he had come into.

The thought lingered sure and strong at the fore of his mind.

This wasn't home. This wasn't Winnipeg.

He knew other worlds existed. His entrance into the Doorway of Darkness taught him that much and his time with Tarek and his encounter with the Bloodans only emphasized it.

With the Bloodans, that world had been entered via a portal made from blood and supernatural evil.

Now . . . now he had come through a veil of black smoke, the same stuff, it seemed, that had come from the Doorway of Darkness. The only question was why didn't the smoke take him back to the realm of Redsaw's master? Was the Doorway of Darkness itself the only means to get there? Wouldn't something from that realm also provide a way back there since, evidently, the black smoke also carried portal-like capabilities?

Or maybe the smoke's mixing with the air, its floating around, changing it somehow? Opened up another *door? And that wasn't just a little smoke that escaped the doorway. There was so much of it it covered the MTS Centre.*

Axiom-man could only hope that much of the smoke had dissipated into the air and whatever hadn't was only confined to that one film of black smoke coating Tom's kid's interior closet wall.

Except he knew better than to wish for a happy ending.

Not now.

Not after the Doorway of Darkness had been opened.

———

Axiom-man stood on Valerie's balcony a long time, the notion that he might not make it home finally sinking in.

I can't give up unless I've exhausted all options. I need to find that cloud—if it exists here—and try and get back home. But before that, I need to find Tom's kid. Something took him. Those streaks on the ground proved that. "But where is he? What took him?"

He slammed his fist down on the balcony railing. The metal squeaked as it bent inward. He didn't care.

The windows of the apartment building across the way were dark and some had wide bloody smudges across the glass. A few of the windows were broken. Only one window looked pristine, out of place in this dead city.

"I got to find that kid," he said. "He's the reason I'm here."

Axiom-man gave one final glance back into the apartment, whispered, "I miss you," then floated into the sky.

He dove toward the city streets, this time when passing by the cars checking for blood. Many of the vehicles were doused in red one way or another. A few, the ones with the broken windows, also carried blotches of dried meat.

For over two hours he checked and re-checked the city. No people. No animals. Every plant was dead.

He finally landed on the roof of the Radisson Hotel and stood on the edge of the building. His mind couldn't wrap itself around the idea that he was totally alone. He couldn't accept it.

Crouching down, Axiom-man took a deep breath. "It's hopeless."

He waited.

His eyes began to droop. He could only imagine what time it was. The temptation to check his watch nearly took him, but he knew that seeing the time would only make things worse. Besides, the time on the watch and the time in this world were probably not the same. All outdoor clocks that Winnipeg had were down anyway so there was no way he could even verify that.

He took a step back from the ledge and started pacing.

A low metallic *boom* thundered below.

He paused, turned, and . . .

Boom.

He jogged to the opposite end of the rooftop, hopped up onto the ledge and perched there, one hand in between his feet to keep himself balanced.

Boom.

To the left.

Boom.

Not far away. Maybe a block or two.

Boom.

Axiom-man dove off the ledge and headed in the direction of the sound.

Boom.

An alleyway not far from the hotel.

He flew down.

Boom.

And flew lower, a few feet off the ground.

He saw the source of the sound.

At the end of the alley a man stood before a dumpster, stepping toward it and slamming his palms up against it, then stepping back, repeating the motion over and over again.

Boom.

The man stepped back, paused, then did it again.

Axiom-man slowed his flight then put his feet down. Slowly, he walked toward the man. The closer he got, the more it was evident this fellow was from the streets. The ratty jeans and torn gray-and-green plaid shirt appeared decades old. The fellow's hair sticking out of the tucked-down black baseball cap was in disarray, a strange mix of brown and gray.

Boom.

The man paused and stared at the dumpster.

Why's he doing that? Axiom-man wondered. *Trying to get at something inside?*

The man stepped back, raised his hands, his wrists limp, then stumbled toward the dumpster and slapped it again.

Axiom-man was almost up to him and the guy didn't seem to acknowledge he was there. The fellow's big, matted beard obscured most of his features.

"Excuse me?" Axiom-man said.

The man took a slow step back then came at the dumpster again.

Boom.

"Do you need help with something?" Axiom-man said.

No answer. The man just stood there before the dumpster.

"Do you know what happened here?"

The guy stood there and didn't move.

Was it Axiom-man's imagination or did the guy ever so slightly turn his head toward him?

Axiom-man closed the distance between them.

"Do you need help?" he asked him slowly.

The man still stood there, staring at the dumpster. The funk of garbage stabbed Axiom-man's nostrils.

"Hey," Axiom-man said and tugged at the guy's shoulder.

When the man turned to face him, the strength ran from Axiom-man's legs.

CHAPTER THREE

THE MAN'S EYES were void of expression, even life. White. They were pure white. No pupils, no irises, not even a hint as to where those things should be. Gray, flaky skin matted his face especially on the cheekbones under his eyes. His dark brown, tangled beard was caked in tiny black-red chunks, as if the guy had shoved his face in a bowl of ground beef.

For a moment, the man merely stared at him, as if this was the first time he had ever laid eyes on another human before.

What was wrong with this guy? Why was his skin like that? Did he have some kind of disease? Is that why he appeared to be homeless, poor and seeking sustenance from a dumpster?

"Are you all—" Axiom-man started but before he could finish the question, the man's arms swung forward in a wild arc and landed on top of his shoulders. The fellow's stern grip went beyond human strength. The last time Axiom-man felt such strong hands upon him was when he and Redsaw had it out at the MTS Centre.

Axiom-man jerked himself away, the man's fingers sliding off his cape. The funk of the man's flesh lingered on the air.

Before Axiom-man could pose another question or even take another step back, the man lurched forward and once again planted his hands on Axiom-man's shoulders, this time harder.

"Hey!" Axiom-man said and shot out both palms into the man's chest.

The man stumbled back with a grunt, bent at the waist, swung his arms side to side to regain his balance, then stood upright again.

"Look, I don't know what you want or what your problem is, but you can't just go around—"

The man dove at him, moving quicker than expected. Gone were the shaky movements and unsure footing. Axiom-man shot up his arms to block the two coming for him, but the man's hands found their way around Axiom-man's defense, latched onto the back of his neck and yanked him forward, slamming the side of his head against the guy's chest.

The man held him there, squeezing, the pressure against the back of his neck growing. If it persisted, the man's hands would squeeze clear through his neck and cut off his air.

Wrestling against him, Axiom-man tried to pull away. Each jerk back only resulted in the man yanking him forward against himself again, as if this were some kind of game. The side of Axiom-man's face rammed up against the fellow's bony ribcage, the stench pouring off the man's clothes that of a landfill.

The man held him there, twisting and turning with each of Axiom-man's moves to the right or left.

"Oww . . ." Axiom-man grunted when the man's grip around his neck increased. Any second now a vertebrae would pop and he'd be in even more trouble.

The man pressed Axiom-man even tighter to his chest, so much so the only thing separating Axiom-man from the man's skin beneath was the man's foul-smelling shirt and the fabric of his own mask. Ear pressed up against the man's chest, Axiom-man noticed the guy's lungs weren't contracting and expanding.

Worse, there was no heartbeat.

Either this guy was holding his breath or Axiom-man's own struggled breathing was muting out the sound.

Or the guy was dead.

It can't be, Axiom-man thought. *Dead people don't move.* But the man's smell and decaying flesh told him otherwise. He was in a world he didn't know and in a city he didn't understand, so it was *possible.*

The man's hold on him increased. It was either act now or never breathe again.

Axiom-man hooked his palms underneath the man's elbows, gripped the joints as tight as he could on either side, and pulled outward, slowly separating the man's hands from his neck. He tucked his chin into his chest, dipped and pulled his body out so he could stand upright again. Still holding the man's arms at bay, Axiom-man had to bend backward to avoid the man's snapping jaws. The ferocious intensity in the man's eyes was almost feral.

This man, whoever he once was, was no longer human.

Not wanting to do any more damage than necessary, Axiom-man shot out his leg and landed a kick square in the man's gut. The force of the blow was enough to knock the guy several feet back. Axiom-man gave a sure push against the man's arms as the guy flew back just for good measure.

He wanted to fly away, rise above this guy and gain some distance, but at the same time he felt compelled to remain, to learn more. What if the whole city was filled with guys like him? What about the world?

Don't get ahead of yourself, Axiom-man thought.

The man stumbled for him again, arms lashing out, grabbing nothing but air, but with each step closer, it'd only be a matter of time before Axiom-man found himself trapped again.

"Stop," Axiom-man said.

The man kept coming. He snapped out his left hand. Axiom-man shoved it away and took a step back.

"I'm serious. Give it up."

Right hand. Axiom-man batted that one away as well, taking note that each block took effort. The guy's strength was amazing and Axiom-man wondered if it matched his own.

No way to know and I really don't want to find out.

The man came at him again, his mouth open wide, yellow teeth worn and chipped ready to bite into him.

"Last warning," Axiom-man said.

The guy didn't seem to care or even hear him. He lurched forward, both hands close together, the space in between his palms perfectly distanced to latch around Axiom-man's neck.

Quickly, Axiom-man allowed blue light to pool in his eyes, his vision temporarily vanishing, as it did each time he allowed the light to fill them, and just as quickly, he sent forth a short burst of blue energy into the man's hands. The guy's hands and fingers exploded in a syrupy gush of gray flesh and black blood the second the blast made contact.

There was no way Axiom-man had given him too much. Even now, with his heart racing, he still had the ability to control his powers under panic.

Axiom-man took a step back. "I didn't mean to . . ."

The guy stood there, looking at his stumps, the wheels behind those dead white eyes turning full steam. Axiom-man didn't think the guy could process what just happened. He himself was having a hard time with it. Normally such a blast would just singe his opponent's skin, a warning shot. Back off or get fried. But the guy's flesh had completely disintegrated. The energy blast seemed to have seared most of the wound shut. Only a few drops of black blood oozed from the injury.

The man dropped his hands then raised them back up again and screeched at the heavens. His throaty growl pierced Axiom-man's ears.

Then he looked at him, white eyes filled with hate.

"I'm warning you, don't make me do that again," Axiom-man said, his voice firm. And, man, did he mean it. He had no patience for those who wouldn't listen. Those who would not stop the violence.

The guy came for him again, arms flailing around and around like a windmill. Axiom-man powered up his eyes and sent another burst into him, this time into his chest. The guy sailed back through the air and crashed into the dumpster, a low metallic bang echoing up and down the alleyway. The man's body slumped to the ground and didn't move.

Unconscious. Good, Axiom-man thought. He eyed the man a moment longer then decided to get off the street and onto a roof. From there, he could think more clearly and plan his next move. Also perhaps see if any others like this guy were out there. He gazed skyward, about to leave the ground.

Movement.

The man rose to his feet. When he turned and faced him, Axiom-man's jaw slackened. A hole about the size of two fists filled the man's chest. Axiom-man could see clear through to the dumpster on the other side.

The man was standing, the place where his heart should be no longer there. Yet the guy was standing!

No breathing. No heartbeat.

This man was dead.

How the thing could move—even growl—Axiom-man didn't know. What he did know was that he couldn't stay here any longer. His own safety aside, the prospect that he was in a city filled with these things made his legs shake with apprehension. He'd seen some pretty strange stuff, encountered creatures not of God's green earth, tossed hands with another man in tights who was more powerful than him—but to see the dead walking . . . this was something entirely new.

The man came for him again, stumps thrown up in an arc then coming down like a pair of sledgehammers.

Axiom-man prepped himself to send one final blast into the man, this time into his legs. That way, he wouldn't be able to move. Before he could, the man's hands came flying down, hammering down onto Axiom-man's shoulders, sending him to his knees. The force of the blow was enough to jolt the power loose from his eyes and the energy blast fired off in the first direction Axiom-man looked. When his vision cleared, the man's headless body dropped to the ground.

Axiom-man shot to his feet, readying himself for the headless corpse to rise again and come after him.

The body didn't move.

"It's over," Axiom-man breathed.

He stood there for several minutes, absorbing what just happened, his ears all the while perked to pick up on the sound of any more that might be coming his way.

The alleyway was quiet and no other sound rose up in the distance.

After taking a deep breath and exhaling slowly, Axiom-man raised his hands toward the sky and floated up to the rooftop overlooking the alley. He went to the edge, leaned over and once more checked the body for movement. Nothing. Just the headless corpse of a homeless man with both his hands missing.

"I didn't mean to kill you," Axiom-man said. He pinched the bridge of his nose as tears pricked at the corners of his eyes. "It was an accident." He took another deep breath and this time held it. He finally exhaled after he walked over to the middle of the roof and began pacing, hands clasped behind his back.

"I couldn't have killed him, right?" he said. "Well, I did, but it was an accident. There's no way I meant to do that on purpose." He paused then continued pacing. "Oh, man, that better be true because we're in big trouble if I'm able to kill without thought, put too much into my power." His heart sped up at the prospect. He replayed it over in his mind. The man; his gray, flaky skin, the white eyes. "No one alive looks like that. And there's not a single disease that makes a person look like that."

He walked to the edge of the building. The body still lay there, chest down.

Back to the middle of the roof. He glanced upward, his vision filled with the murky gray of a dead sky.

Yeah. Everything's dead. The man was already dead. He moved when he didn't have a heart. I heard no heartbeat. I heard no *heartbeat!*

He paced back to the edge of the building and looked over once more. A jolt hit him in the chest when he understood what was going on: "The dead have risen from the grave."

CHAPTER FOUR

AXIOM-MAN FLEW OVER the city, the streets below slowly unveiling shadowy, shambling figures. Wherever they had been hiding not long before, they had now come out and, it seemed, were looking for something.

He allowed himself to fly low enough to get a good look at them—all with gray or yellow-tainted faces, those milky white eyes, filthy clothes, each smelling like garbage with a hint of curdled milk—but remained high enough that, should they look up, there would be no way they could reach up and grab him. With each pass closer to the ground, he kept an eye out for Tom's boy. Once more he shook his head at his stupidity for not knowing the kid's name or even what the boy looked like. The only way he'd find him was to find a kid who wasn't one of the dead. But even then, if there were others out there who were alive, who's to say that a "living boy" wasn't just that: a living boy? It might not even be Tom's kid.

Don't get too wrapped up in it, Axiom-man told himself. *One thing at a time.*

With each hour that passed, more and more of the dead came out of the shadows, the alleys, the buildings with broken windows and busted-up doors. Soon they littered the streets like ants crawling around an anthill.

"He could be anywhere down there," Axiom-man said. "Obviously one of those things took him. But as to *where* it took him is anyone's guess. There has to be some way to know or something to tip me off. If the kid isn't dead already, that is. The way that thing attacked me . . ." He paused. "Dead and moving though they are, they're not that bright. That thing kept coming after me even after I shot his hands off and blasted a hole through his chest. Something else drives them. Something else does their thinking for them."

Axiom-man hovered in the air, resolving not to set down unless he had to or saw something that would help him find the boy.

Time went on.

He kept his eyes on the streets; the dead filled the pavement, a horde of decaying bodies and shuffling feet.

So many people, so many faces. A sharp and hollow pang struck his heart. These were the same people, in his world, that he fought for day in and day out. Now, here, they were all dead. And some down there, he knew, some could be those he loved: his mom, his dad, his brother. Even his coworkers could be down there, walking about in the sea of the dead. Even Valerie.

I hope she's okay. I hope she's alive.

It wasn't long before he couldn't take it anymore so he flew over the streets, searching them for any sign of the living. He stuck to what many considered the main stretch of downtown, flying over from the main hub of Portage and Main all the way down to Polo Park and back. He surveyed the side streets and flew low to check the windows of some of the houses and apartment buildings for those who might still be alive.

Now near the Forks, he flew along the Assiniboine River, eyeing the path alongside it. Maybe, if someone was alive, they'd come here, near the water. Odds were the dead couldn't swim. You could take a boat on the river and be safe. But if you fell in, the undertow would end you.

Nowhere's safe anymore.

The Forks was where the Assiniboine met the Red River, the one place in the city shared by all without reserve, a common ground to celebrate special occasions like Canada Day or merely just to take your family for an afternoon in the sun. Shops bordered the main square there—the Johnston Terminal, the Citytv Building, the viewing tower—and Axiom-man hoped someone would be here.

Anyone.

The viewing tower.

Though it had been several months now, it was a beacon to a turning point in his relationship with Valerie. He had saved her one day after she had fallen through a hole in the side railing of the Main Street Bridge, the same day Redsaw was there and accidentally killed a young man named Gene Nemek, who had been a trainee at Dollacard at the time.

Axiom-man flew toward the tower. As he neared it, something moving behind the glass-enclosed staircase caught his eye. At first they were mere shadows, but the closer he got, the more their dark forms became clearer. Not knowing what might happen should they belong to those of the dead, he readied himself for anything and prepared to let the blue light fill his eyes so, if need be, he could send an explosive blast through the glass. But these people didn't move like the dead. There was no stumbling in their steps. Though each had a hand to the railing as they climbed the stairs to the top of the viewing deck, they moved up the steps with relative ease. Closer now and he saw that they were human. Elderly. A man and a woman.

Not sure if this world had its own Axiom-man and if these folks were accustomed to seeing a man flying around, he took off high into the sky and positioned himself several hundred feet above and slightly behind the viewing deck, hovered, and waited for the two to emerge from the stairwell. When they did, he watched and waited, to see what they might do.

The two elderly folks stepped out onto the deck. One of them carried something long and dark. From this high up, he couldn't tell if it was the man or the woman.

Gotta get closer.

Keeping his distance, Axiom-man lowered himself so he came up right behind the viewing deck, keeping in line with the greeny-blue metal beams that composed the structure. Staying close to the beam, but not touching it— blotches of dried, light gray paint covered it—he peered around its corner at the couple. They reminded him of his grandparents. Better, these folks were *alive.*

Finally. People who were alive.

Both of them wore thick fall coats, the man's navy blue, the woman's brown. Each had short gray hair that stuck out from beneath a pair of matching red winter hats, the kind with floppy ears and a fuzzy pom-pom on top. It wasn't freezing so Axiom-man assumed the winter-esque clothing was an effort to protect themselves against the dead.

The man had a rifle. Looked like an old .22.

Off to the side, down below, hoarse bellows sifted on the air.

The dead were coming. At first, only a few shuffled their way across the main square, moving toward the viewing tower. Soon, they were joined by others, many of whom came from under the bridge at the side of the Forks and the trees that lined the river next to the path.

"There they are again, Elise," the man said, leaning over the railing that rimmed the deck, his old voice carrying the blunt edge of defeat.

"Stop saying that!" Elise said. "You say that every time you see one of those things."

"There's not just 'one of those things' down there. There's about fifty of 'em. Fifty. Stan said there'd maybe be ten, a dozen at most, when he called us out here."

Elise crossed her arms. "Maybe Stan was wrong."

The man harrumphed. "Or maybe he didn't know what he was talking about? When was the last time *you* were outside? A month? Two?"

She shook her head.

"Me, too," he said and came over to her, putting a hand on her shoulder. "I lost count as well."

They both leaned over the railing and watched as more and more of the dead rallied around the base of the viewing tower, their blank white gazes staring upward, perhaps trying to figure out a way to get up there and destroy these two old folks who were apparently waiting for a guy named Stan.

"What time did he say he'd come, Peter?" Elise asked.

Peter set the butt of the rifle on the ground, leaned it up against his belly, and rolled back the cuff of his jacket, checking his watch. "He said 11:30. It's 11:34."

"He's late."

"I know that, Elise."

She shot him a cool look.

His eyes softened and he gave a warm smile. "Sorry."

Axiom-man's ears perked up again when another round of raspy cries rose from below. The dead surrounded the ground floor in front and along each side of the viewing tower. To the right, many were coming from up the paved hill that led to Main Street. A few of the shambling corpses lost their footing when descending the hill and tumbled down, knocking into others, bringing even more to the ground. The ones around those that fell just kept walking, not missing a beat, their eyes fixed forward, heading toward the tower.

"Do you think they'll get inside?" Elise asked.

"I don't know," Peter said. "I've seen them bang down doors; I've seen them stand before doors, not knowing what to do. Some are smarter than others, it seems."

"Where's Stan?"

Peter took a deep breath and exhaled slowly. "Wish I knew."

"We can't stay up here."

"I know."

"Ten more minutes then we go home."

"What about the meat?"

"We can live without it. We have been for the past several weeks."

"It's important, Elise. The fruits and vegetables are almost gone. What we got left is all in cans. You need protein. Meat's good for that. I'm sick of beans."

Elise stepped back from the railing. "We got a couple of eggs, some peanut butter."

Peter chuckled. "So we'll have an egg-and-peanut-butter sandwich? Mmm. Can't wait."

The old woman smiled. "I love you."

"I love you, too."

Axiom-man couldn't help but smile himself. He hoped he'd have someone like Elise once he got to Peter's age; someone who could laugh even when the going got tough.

The dead cried out below and the first line of them stomped toward the windows at the base of the viewing tower and slapped their palms up against them. The low drumming of each bang rattled the glass and sent a series of thumps echoing throughout Axiom-man's ribcage.

Peter raised the rifle and leaned over the edge, aiming to take a shot.

"You don't have enough bullets!" Elise said.

He turned and eyed the door leading to the stairwell. "We can go back the way we came in. Out past the fruit market."

"What if they've blocked that entrance, too?"

"Then we're in trouble."

The dead growled, groaned and beat against the glass.

Peter and Elise peered over the railing again.

More and more of the dead came and filled the square in front of the viewing tower and the Forks Market Building. All exits seemed to be blocked. Axiom-man knew which one Peter was referring to, the one past the fruit and vegetable stand. From where he hovered behind the beam, he couldn't see if it was blocked as well.

Glass shattered below as the dead broke through.

"They're coming," Peter said.

The dead poured into the building.

"We need to go," Elise said.

"It's too late. They'll find the stairs and come up here. Even if we did manage to get down, they'd already be clogging the hallways, blocking the exits. You know how your knees get on stairs."

"Then we're trapped."

Peter nodded and tears wet his eyes.

Axiom-man floated around to the side of the tower and perched on the railing. "Maybe I can help."

CHAPTER FIVE

THE OLD MAN staggered back a step. Elise reached out and caught him by the elbow so he wouldn't lose his balance.

"You . . ." Peter was barely able to get the words out.

Disbelief and a hint of skepticism were written across both of their faces.

Axiom-man had seen this kind of reaction before, the shock and sheer strangeness of seeing a man in a costume for the first time, and not just a man in a costume, but one who had the ability to do things no one else could. But that wasn't what concerned him about Peter and Elise's reaction. Peter had said, "You."

Was it possible that this place—*this* Winnipeg—had an Axiom-man, too?

"Sir—" Axiom-man started but was quickly cut off.

"You're supposed to be dead," Peter said.

"Taken," Elise added. "By *them.*"

Axiom-man struggled to put a palm up to silence them. He had so many questions. "Listen, I don't have time to explain, but you two need to come with me otherwise those things will get you." He hopped down off the railing and stood beside them.

Elise and Peter took a few more steps back, Peter bumping up against the corner railing of the viewing deck.

"I'm not going to hurt you," Axiom-man said. He held out his hand. "You both need to come with me."

The low drum of footfalls on the hollow cement steps echoed in the stairwell leading up to the viewing tower. Deep, guttural growls filled the air.

Peter looked to Elise, as if seeking her permission to trust this stranger in a cape.

She leaned in and whispered to him, "Could be him, maybe not. He appeared on the railing and you and I both know there were only two in this city who could fly before the rain came."

The old man eyed Axiom-man coolly. His expression changed, as if he was more concerned with the man in blue before them than the walking corpses making their way up the stairs.

You need to trust me, Axiom-man thought. *You're getting a few more seconds then I'm taking you both out of here whether you like it or not.*

He turned his head in the direction of the stairwell. The creatures weren't that far away.

The shuffling footfalls were getting louder.

Peter picked up his rifle and examined it. To Elise: "Stan's not coming, is he?"

Elise slowly shook her head. "I don't think so."

The old man hefted his rifle then brought it up stomach height. To Axiom-man: "I guess we don't have a choice."

"No, you don't," Axiom-man said just as a pack of the creatures made it to the top of the stairs.

The diseased faces of men and women, old and young, filled in behind the glass door leading onto the viewing deck. They stopped a moment and eyed their prey. One caught Axiom-man's eye: a man, probably mid-thirties, with half of his gray face peeled away, exposing the rotting flesh beneath, a white eyeball with a white iris floating in its socket. The man's eyes bore into him, perplexity yet a *knowingness* of what to do deep within his gaze.

Axiom-man stepped close to Peter and Elise and opened his arms. "Each take a side and wrap your arms around my waist. Even hold onto each other, if you have to. I'm going to have to grip you hard, so that's just a warning."

The glass door pulsed a low *badoom* when the man with the peeled-back face slammed his palms against it. The door shook in its hinges.

Suddenly springing into action, Peter and Elise huddled up against Axiom-man and hugged him around the waist, squeezing a lot tighter than he had expected them to, so much so that it was difficult to breathe.

No matter. Just get them out of here and—

CRASH! The glass of the door shattered and the creatures poured onto the viewing deck, each seeming not to care when their already-torn clothes caught on the jagged bits of glass rimming the doorframe. They piled in, some getting through no problem, others falling over each other, seemingly unable to wait their turn to get to the three people at the far corner of the viewing deck.

"Hold on," Axiom-man said and took a tight hold on each of the old folks' shoulders.

His feet left the ground and he headed upward.

Just as he was about to clear the railing and fly the two to safety, gray scaly fingers grabbed hold of his cape and yanked him downward.

"Look out!" Elise shouted as Axiom-man's body torqued to the side from the sudden catch on his cape.

"Let go!" Peter shouted at the monsters below.

Axiom-man fought against their pull and was able to get a few more feet of air when a quick jerk yanked him back toward the viewing deck. Many more must have grabbed onto his cape. He looked back over his shoulder and saw the creatures working together against them, some pulling down on his cape, others tugging at those who were doing the pulling, adding to their strength.

Grunting, he ascended but not before a tall creature got a strong hand around his foot and jerked him back and downward.

The creatures wrapped their fingers around Peter and Elise and drew them back onto the viewing deck. One hooked a forearm around Axiom-man's neck from behind, cutting off his air completely. Peter and Elise's increased hold around his middle put pressure on his ribs and he feared that if they squeezed any harder, one or more of his ribs might break. They needed to let go, but if they did . . .

The two elderly people screamed as the creatures pulled them away from him despite his trying to keep them close to himself.

They're so strong, he thought absentmindedly.

Peter and Elise were yanked free and both screamed as they were absorbed by the mass of monsters crowding the viewing tower.

Something thick and hard bashed against the back of Axiom-man's skull, snapping his head forward, his neck collapsing as he bent over the forearm squeezing his trachea.

Need air, he thought. His head began to buzz and his eyes hurt. *That's it. Just let loose.*

He reached up and curled his fingers around the creature's forearm, ripping it away in one powerful pull. Taking a deep breath, he spun around and clocked the monster across the face, sending the thing spinning like a top on its feet and tumbling over the railing. A few seconds later its body smacked the stone-covered ground below, splatting open like a melon.

Taking a quick peek over the heads of dead men and women, his heart cried out at the sight of Elise and Peter separated. They struggled against the creatures while looking toward each other in one last loving gesture of good-bye.

"You're not going to die!" Axiom-man shouted to them, though, above the growls and groans of the creatures, he wasn't sure if they heard him.

Grimacing, rage exploding within, he lashed out, slamming a fist in an uppercut under the jaw of one of the creatures, sending it sailing into the air and over the railing. He dipped down, grabbed the shins of another and hoisted it upward. The thing only got two slaps of the palm to his back before it was tossed over the railing to join its comrades below.

Giving in to the anger building within, Axiom-man let blue light fill his eyes, its immense energy blanketing his vision in glorious blue-white, the crackle of its power a song to his ears.

He let go with everything he had, firing off blast after blast into the creatures, zapping through the heads of some, leaving burn holes straight through the skulls in their wake, others enough of a blast to cleave their heads off at the neck.

The bodies dropped like flies.

Now with some distance between him and them, he tore off from the ground and flew above the heads of the creatures, heading first to Elise, who bashed against the monsters with the sides of her fists.

The old woman was in hysterics, crying and screaming, her voice already raw from the exertion.

"I got you," Axiom-man said and landed beside her.

BANG!

Not far away, Peter shot off a creature's face. "Get out of here, Elise! Don't worry about me!"

"I'm not leaving you!" she screamed.

Axiom-man punched one of the creatures in the head so hard his fist buried into its skull, black blood and brain splashing onto his gloves. He shot his foot in between the legs of another, lodging his boot into a mash of flesh and bone. He withdrew his foot, powered up his eyes, and blasted away three more.

Quickly, he grabbed Elise and flew over to Peter.

The old man was on his knees, two creatures clawing at him. One set of a monster's long cracked fingernails sliced into his neck, leaving a smooth trail of four lines of blood.

"Give me your hand," Axiom-man said, reaching down as he floated over him.

Peter glanced up with watery eyes.

Something grabbed Axiom-man's foot, trying to bring him down. It was only one creature. Axiom-man raised his knee, dragged up the creature's body with it, then snapped it outward, kicking the creature off and over the railing.

An old shaky hand surfaced amongst the throng of the dead.

Axiom-man grabbed it, pulled and zipped into the sky as fast he could, Elise at his side, Peter dangling by the hand at his knees.

The remaining creatures shrieked and groaned on the viewing deck, watching in bewilderment as Axiom-man and the two others drifted away into the murky gray sky.

Elise screamed.

"It's okay. I've got you. You're not going to fall," Axiom-man said as assuringly as possible.

Sniffling, she said, "Peter . . ."

Axiom-man looked down.

The bottoms of Peter's legs were missing.

Chapter Six

Elise immediately squeezed Axiom-man around the sides, nothing but passion and grief emanating from her hold.

Peter's grip began to slip.

"Hold on," Axiom-man said, unable to take his eyes off the remnants of Peter's legs.

Blood dripped from the torn fleshy stumps, one leg ripped at the knees, the other shredded at mid thigh. The crimson droplets dribbled like a weak rain to the gray-washed streets below.

"No . . . oh no . . ." Elise sobbed, her voice quiet.

Peter hung there, head bowed, limp, the only indication that he wasn't completely dead the subtle grip he still had on Axiom-man's hand, his other still hanging onto the rifle. Axiom-man tightened his fingers around the old man's.

"Is there a hospital . . . is there something still . . ." Axiom-man said.

Elise shook her head, sniffled. "Empty." She swallowed a tear-filled lump. "Can you hear me, Peter? Can you—"

The old man weakly looked up. His eyes were glazed over, but there was no sign of pain on his face. His blank, glassy stare read shock and shock alone.

Axiom-man didn't know where he was going to take them. There was no one who could help them and the streets below, dotted with the shambling forms of the creatures, were no place to set down. A rooftop, maybe?

Elise spoke to Peter; it sounded like German and Axiom-man didn't understand her. Language of the old country.

The poor fella just hung there, chin once more pressed against his chest, every few seconds his grip getting weaker and weaker until Axiom-man was the one doing the holding. The old man still had his rifle though.

Tears rolling down Elise's cheeks, she didn't take her eyes off her husband.

"It's over," she said.

Axiom-man didn't understand. "It's over?"

"He's . . . he's almost gone."

"I'm sorry."

She didn't reply.

Heart aching for her, a longing to comfort her beginning to take hold, Axiom-man wished to whisper words of reassurance. But something else brewed beneath the sadness: anger. He should have acted more quickly on the viewing tower. Should have just simply unleashed the power he held, entrusted to him by the nameless messenger who visited him one night and bestowed upon him his abilities. Instead he handled it like a novice.

Never again.

Doing his best to not show any emotion, Axiom-man said, "We can't fly on forever. Is there someplace I can take him? Take us?"

Elise buried her head in her sleeve and wiped her eyes. "There's no place for him now."

The rifle dropped and was sucked to the streets below.

Peter's hand went limp; Axiom-man latched on, squishing the old man's fingers between his own.

"You need to let go," she said.

Did she just say . . . "Let go?"

"You have to. In a few moments, Peter will return but it won't be him." Then, with pleading eyes, she added, "You have to believe me. I know you wouldn't . . . I know you wouldn't do this, but you have to."

"I can't do that," he said. "Just because he—"

"No. It's not like that. Peter's dead. I know that's what you mean, but now . . . now my sweet husband will return as one of them."

She was serious. She really did want him to let go of the body and let it fall.

Everything that made up who he was told him she was crazy, that she was speaking out of grief and panic. Yet the earnestness with which she spoke tugged at his heart strings and was making him believe otherwise.

"Do it," she said, her voice breaking.

"Ma'am, I—"

Peter's fingers inside his palm suddenly went rigid and just as quickly reaffirmed their grip on his hand. A grip of steel.

"Do it!" Elise shouted.

Peter's head arced back on his neck, white eyes bulging, mouth open, bloody and syrupy saliva ropes connecting top and bottom lips.

Axiom-man jolted.

A low growl spilled from behind the old man's teeth.

"Drop him!" she screamed.

Peter began pulling himself up toward them with one arm, mouth open, his face heading for Axiom-man's arm.

Axiom-man let go.

Peter still held on, dropped a few inches, then began pulling himself back up.

Elise kicked at her husband's body, the tip of her shoe connecting with the side of his head, sending his face off course and buying Axiom-man some time.

"Drop him! Drop him!" she screamed, her voice zapping straight into Axiom-man's ear, sending off a high-pitched ring in his head.

Never again . . . He filled his eyes with blue energy, blanketing Peter's hanging form, transforming him to shadow against the light.

CRACK!

The beam shot forth, slicing into Peter's arm, severing it at the elbow.

The old man fell; he didn't scream, just cast a lost white stare as if he didn't really know what happened at all.

A second later, the dismembered hand in Axiom-man's own relaxed. Axiom-man let it go to fall and join its owner.

Elise buried her face into Axiom-man's shoulder and wept.

"I'm sorry," he said, raising his head to face the horizon, one coated in gray clouds mixed with dark brown.

The elderly woman didn't reply.

She just squeezed him harder.

———

"It started around four months ago," Elise said as she sat in an old, green chair embroidered with flowers made from gold thread.

The way she sat there in the dim light by the window reminded Axiom-man of the Marsch residence when he first entered this world.

Elise held a mug of tea tightly between old and wrinkled fingers, her jacket still on. The tea was cold, but she had wanted it anyway despite the power having gone out from her and Peter's tiny home just outside downtown only yesterday. While she made the tea she said they had used a generator for power because most of the city had already gone out not long after everything changed. Only a few places still had the lights on, she said.

Axiom-man had let her work at her own pace and only when she took her tea into the living room and sat in the antique chair did he stand in front of her, facing away, and began asking questions.

The first was what happened.

"I remember that day," Elise said, her voice still weak and grief-stricken. "It was late afternoon. Peter and I were preparing supper when suddenly our kitchen grew dark. The light coming in the window turned to shadow as immense gray clouds covered the sky in a matter of seconds." She took a loud sip of her tea. "Then it began to rain. We watched it come down just over there." Axiom-man turned to see her nodding in the direction of the panoramic window in the living room that overlooked the front street. "It was gray rain, like old tin cans without their labels. It covered everything. It wasn't long before we heard screams coming from not too far away, their sound so loud we heard it in here through the window. The tires squealing, the children shrieking. Cars crashing."

She blew on her tea, presumably out of habit, and took another sip. "Then we saw the people. So many of them walking past our house, soaked to the bone, all seemingly lost and completely unaware of where to go. Peter wanted to go outside to help but I stopped him. I told him those walking by didn't look quite right and it wasn't that they were simply all covered head to toe in gray." Her voice grew quieter. "It was the way they walked. Slow, so uneven. The jerky movements."

Axiom-man crossed his arms and faced away again. "How long did it rain for?"

"A week. A whole week, and if I remember correctly, it was exactly a week, the rain finally stopping late afternoon seven days later."

"When did you finally go outside?"

"We weren't supposed to. No one was. The TV was still running and every news channel from all over covered the same story."

All for Winni—

"In every city. In every country."

The whole world. Axiom-man's insides sank.

"There were reports of attacks. Those that had been caught out in the rain were changed somehow. It was from the TV we heard that they . . ." He turned to face her. When his eyes settled on hers, she looked away. The next words out of her mouth were barely audible. "That they ate people."

Then it's true, he thought. He shouldn't have been surprised, not with all that he'd experienced since having his powers, but the news still shook him nonetheless.

Zombies.

They were real.

"It was just an issue of surviving after that." She put the rim of the cup between her lips and just kept it there, as if it might stop her from saying anything more, from going down a path of memory that she might never return from.

Axiom-man let the quiet of the house remain on the air for several moments, a chance for Elise and himself to process all that happened.

He took a few steps closer to her and did his best to speak as gently as possible; he didn't want to disrespect her grief. "Your husband told me I was supposed to be dead. What did he mean by that?"

Elise looked up from her cup. "He meant just what he said. You're supposed to be dead."

CHAPTER SEVEN

Elise's expression changed. The sadness in her eyes was blinked away and in its place came a look of intense curiosity and . . . hope.

"How did you escape them?" she asked.

"Them? The—"

"The dead."

The dead. Zombies. Axiom-man shook his head. "I didn't escape them."

She took another sip of tea. She clearly didn't believe him. "Yes, you did. You saved me and Pe—and Peter." The sadness returned.

A sharp pang pierced his heart. "I didn't save him," he whispered.

"Pardon?"

"Your husband. I'm . . . I'm sorry. I'm sorry I didn't save him."

She glanced away. "You tried."

It was quiet again.

Elise set the teacup down on the small polished wooden table beside the chair. "You came for us. You escaped them."

"No, I didn't. I'm not from here, Elise."

She perked up at the statement. It was the first time he addressed her by name and most folks experienced a little jolt every time he did so solely because of who he was.

"What do you mean? Right after the rain, you and Redsaw set aside your differences and joined together to stand against them."

Redsaw and I . . . No, it couldn't be true. After that night in the Doorway of Darkness, it was determined that Redsaw was now out for the kill, that Redsaw needed him out of the way to fulfill the promise of rule given in that realm of red and black cloud. To think that that suddenly didn't matter to Redsaw, that his thirst for power could suddenly cease even due to such an enormous crisis—Axiom-man knew him better than that. He knew they were destined to war until one of them emerged victorious.

He came even closer to her. He must have moved suddenly because she sat straight up in her chair, alarm on her face. "Where is he? Where's Redsaw?"

"Dead," she said.

"You thought the same of me."

"No, he's dead. They overcame him and . . ."

"And?"

The muscles beneath her wrinkled skin grew hard. "And ripped him to pieces."

Axiom-man eased off and gave her some room.

She continued. "His body was shown on the news before the cable went out. The pieces. I dare not describe it. You were there, standing over what was left of his body. Don't you remember?"

He raised a finger. "Elise, listen to me. I wasn't there. I'm not from here. The Axiom-man you saw wasn't me."

"What are you saying? Where are you from, then?"

"Not here. I came by accident. I . . ." *I don't even know how I'm going to get back. If I'm going to get back.* "I came looking for someone. A boy. Seven years old. I don't know his first name. His last name is Marsch. You don't know anybody by that name, do you?"

Axiom-man knew full well that she didn't, that there was no way for the kid's name to be known between the time the boy was taken to the time he came here through the portal in his bedroom. It just didn't hurt to ask.

"No," she said.

He nodded.

"Maybe you just don't remember. Maybe they did something to you and either you escaped or they let you go and you can't recall what happened."

"For the final time, it's not me who you're talking about."

"It doesn't make sense."

"I know." Even he was having a hard time grasping the idea of there being *two* of him. Worse, *two* of Redsaw. He could only imagine the carnage that would have ensued had the Redsaw from here had somehow gotten to his world. If the two Redsaws had teamed up, there would be no telling what might have happened. There would have been no way to stand against them.

None.

"Are you sure you don't remember?"

She wasn't getting it. He was still having a hard time with it. The idea of crossing over between worlds— parallel dimensions—still took his breath away and made his heart speed in his chest even after it having already happened twice before now.

He didn't think it wise to let Elise in on everything. The poor woman had already been through so much today.

"If I don't remember," he said, cringing inside at playing along and intentionally misleading her, "what happened to me? Do you know?"

She picked up the teacup again and held it before her mouth. She blew across its rim. "No specifics, just that it was said on the radio that you had disappeared and all that was found was a portion of your cape, ripped and covered in blood. When you didn't resurface and when there were no reports of one of the dead looking or behaving like you—you know, what you can do—then we presumed the worst." She sipped her tea. "You need to come forward. You need to tell someone, someone in charge, that you're okay. You can help fix this. There's so many of them—everywhere—and already our military failed. They're failing worldwide as we speak." Her eyes bore into his. "You have to say something."

He turned away and glanced to the floor, the heaviness within settling anew. If he didn't find the kid, if he didn't make it home, he'd have no choice but to do something. Standing up for those who couldn't stand up for themselves was his charge. It was why he chose to do what he did because he knew what it was like in his former life to be overlooked, shoved aside and be uncared for.

"In time." He faced her. "I need to find that boy, Elise."

"He's dead."

"You don't know that."

"Oh, I know that. Those things take you and either eat you or make you one of them. There have been no survivors."

"You survived."

"You saved me."

"I have to try. I need to. I'm not going to give up."

She crossed her legs, tears wetting her eyes. She was no doubt thinking about Peter. "Okay, then. Then try."

"Is there anything you can tell me that I might be able to use? I've already flown over the city, looking for him. If he's inside somewhere, it would take forever to search every building, every house."

"The concert hall," she said.

"The concert hall?"

"They've been seen going in there. They live downtown, but it's there that they tend to filter through. That's all I can tell you. That's all I know."

"Does anyone else know this?"

"Everyone does, but all who have tried to infiltrate the place were either killed upon entering or never seen again. Scouts, who monitored the efforts, saw everything."

"Couldn't they have bombed it?"

"The resources to do so were gone by then and those who did try were just everyday folks who wanted to take their city back. And they're all dead or one of the dead."

He stood up straight. "Then I will try. It's the only chance of finding the boy."

"It was probably where they took you. Are you sure you want to go back?"

Axiom-man strode over to the window and parted the semi-transparent curtains. Outside, the street was empty, the gray and brown sky shading everything in murky gray light. "I'm sure."

———

Axiom-man had checked with her several times if she would be all right, if she wanted him to come back after he was done if she needed to talk about Peter.

"I don't want you to come back," she said. "I don't want you worrying about me when you have more important things to do. Maybe one day, once this is over, you can come and say hello. But not today. Or tomorrow or the next."

She stood in her doorway as she watched him glide off the front step and float into the air.

"Thank you, Elise," he said. "I'll do right by you and Peter today."

She nodded. "I know you will." She wiped the tears from her eyes.

With gentleness in his eyes, Axiom-man raised his hand and waved good-bye then flew away.

Elise turned, closed the door behind her, and faced her empty house. Even though she knew better, she expected Peter to come from the other room and wrap his arms around her. Let her know she made the right choice telling Axiom-man where he could find the dead despite it being a death sentence.

But she knew better.

She locked the door and went back to the chair. Before picking up her teacup, she rolled back her sleeve, revealing three long scratches rimmed with black blood.

It was different for everyone, but it would only be a matter of time before the change took hold.

CHAPTER EIGHT

BELOW, THE DEAD roamed the streets, some seeming to walk with purpose, their limping strides taking them to a place only they knew. Others just stood there, gazing at the empty cars, each examining them as if they were trying to recall what they did with the vehicles back when they had been alive. Others stood in front of building windows, lost in their own reflections.

Axiom-man kept his distance, flying high enough between the buildings to remain unnoticed but not so high as not to see all that was going on below.

He headed directly for Main Street but not before doing an about-face mid air and sailing through the sky when an ear-piercing scream rocked him to his core. Below, at an intersection in the Exchange District, a horde of zombies were gathered in a loose circle, looming over the kicking and screaming body of a young woman. When Axiom-man was nearly upon them, eyes already powered up, the screaming ceased. He let the blue light leave his eyes so he could see, only to be greeted by the satisfied groans of the dead and the wet popping sounds of the young woman's body being torn apart, her torso dropping to the pavement once her head and appendages had been removed.

Flashes of Peter hanging limply by his old, frail hand as he attempted to fly the elderly man to safety from earlier danced before his mind.

He had been too late to save him. He hadn't acted efficiently on the viewing deck.

He hadn't found the kid.

He was without a way home.

Blood pounding through his veins, anger storming his heart and soaking every muscle, Axiom-man growled and, fists clenched, sped toward them. He righted himself just above the center of their gathering, powering up his eyes full blast as he descended into the midst of them. The moment his feet touched the ground, he spun around, letting loose all that was pent up within, anger and rage dictating the ferocity of sheer power streaming forth from his eyes, slicing through the zombies like an enormous saw blade through hundreds of pounds of raw meat.

Gurgled moans quickly sprang to life, then just as quickly were silenced as he sent the creatures back to hell where they belonged.

His cape whirled around his ankles when he slowed his spin and stopped. Black blood from the dismembered and decapitated bodies pooled around his feet.

He didn't move but instead stood there, surveying their distorted and torn remains, the poor woman's torso.

No mercy. Not anymore. Not to these things.

They were dead. He was just finishing the job.

Grimacing, he pointed his still-clenched fists skyward and took to the sky, kicking on the speed and riding the adrenaline straight to the concert hall. If the place was like Elise said, if it was where the dead gathered, he would make them pay for what they did to Peter, for taking the boy, for killing that girl.

Today, the eradication of evil deserved no restraint.

He landed on the roof of the concert hall and hopped over to the ledge and looked over it.

The corpses roamed the street out front, some bumping into each other, others walking in curving lines. A few must have noticed him slaughtering their kin because they stood there, gazing up at him.

The concrete canopies that hung over the tinted-black windows that covered the front of the concert hall like a checkerboard were washed in fading gray, the dried remnants of that awful rain Elise talked about. The entire city was covered with the stuff, each building cracked and dry and washed out like some kind of enormous graveyard.

A dead land.

This wasn't the city Axiom-man knew and it shook him to the core; if he wasn't careful in his own universe, his Winnipeg could wind up the same. So much responsibility was placed on him. Not only did the people look up to him, but he was all that stood between Winnipeg and Redsaw.

If he erred, if he somehow let go of the control entrusted to him—chaos. Death.

Hell.

Then you can start by redeeming things here, by finding the boy. Old Tom's counting on you. Gunn will see to it you leave the city if you screw this up. Getting back to my world or not, I have to find that kid.

Slowing his breathing by inhaling through his nose, he crouched down and put a hand to the building's roof. A gentle vibration tingled into his palm. Movement inside.

"They're here," he said, stood, then ran off the ledge and floated to the first window from the rooftop.

He put his ear to the glass.

Moans. Grumblings. Growls.

The haunting calls of the dead drifted from the window and ran through him like a soft breeze. Despite his racing heart, he used the new surge of adrenaline coursing through him like a battery and floated back from the window, shot out his arms, clenched his fists, and flew straight through the glass, emerging on the other side into the concert hall's spacious unlit lobby.

Shuffling feet scraped against the tiled flooring below. He couldn't see them nor did he need to.

Not yet.

Wet slurping sounds wafted up, reminding him of a pack of dogs chowing down on slippery meat.

It had been a long time since he'd been to the concert hall. The last was for *The Phantom of the Opera* back when he was in grade school. But he thought he remembered the overall layout of the place.

Have to clear the room, he thought.

Blue light filled his eyes, casting a gorgeous cobalt hue onto the room. It was almost beautiful, if not for the decaying dead faces it revealed below. The energy in his eyes built and built and eventually cut off his sight so all he saw was the glorious blue-white that was his power.

He let that power fly, blasting it into the walls, the floor, the chandeliers.

Each blast erupted in flame, bathing the room in the bright yellows and orange of a fire gone wild.

The enormous lamps fell from their holdings, crashing onto the ground in an explosion of gold-plated metal and crystal, squishing some of the dead.

Many of the zombies looked up; a few furrowed their brows, as if they understood what was going on, their white stares filled with malicious intent.

Powering up his eyes again, Axiom-man flew over them, discharging blast after blast of blue energy into the shambling corpses, blowing them to bits in sprays of blood, brain and floppy limbs.

The funk of the dead filled the place, its rotten-fish smell mixing in with the sharp tang of dark gray smoke gushing from the walls.

Blast after blast. More power. More energy. Axiom-man flew back and forth across the lobby, losing himself in their destruction, paying them back for killing Peter and for bringing him here to a place he could not escape from.

For taking him from Valerie.

He flew low, brought his elbows in so his fists and forearms were parallel to the floor like a battering ram. He plowed through the dead, knowing full well his ripping through them tore through their bodies like a BMW gone off the road, bowling through anything in its path.

The guttural cries of the dead echoed throughout the room, overriding the roars of the flames.

In the smoky orange glow, Axiom-man was surprised to see there were still so many—packs of them—all trying to track his swift movement like a pack of dogs following a dangling piece of meat.

This was the hub.

He could only imagine what was behind the main doors that led into the concert hall itself.

He doubled back, plowing through another horde of corpses, eyes letting go every ounce of energy he could come up with, cutting through them, severing heads from bodies.

Blood splashed over him in a series of waves, quickly soaking into his uniform and coating his skin. He clamped his mouth shut beneath his mask so he wouldn't accidentally swallow any.

He reached the far wall of the lobby, banked against it, then set his heels on the wall and kicked off, this time flying even lower, the energy from his eyes cutting off the dead below the knees.

Thudthudthudthudthud.

Thudthudthudthudthud.

They dropped fast and sure, their dead bodies hitting the ground in hollow thunks, plasticy skulls slapping the tiles and carpeting.

Whoosh.

Flames erupted behind him.

He didn't care.

A sharp pain pierced his back and what felt like a pair of steel hands slammed against his shoulder blades, plowing him into the floor. He skidded across the ground, the friction blasting searing heat into his chest, igniting his skin beneath his suit.

Axiom-man rammed into a pack of zombies like a car crashing into a lamppost, wrapping himself around one of their legs. The creature reached down, picked him up by the back of the cape and immediately brought its jaws to the back of his neck. Eyes still to the floor, unable to see his attacker's face, Axiom-man reached out with his left hand and found the creature's stomach. He pulled his arm back then launched it forward, ramming his fist through the creature's black turtleneck and into the soft, gooey gut beyond. His fingers wrapped around the monster's intestines and he ripped them out; sloppy strings slick with fat and blood, like thick noodles with too much sauce. The creature pulled its head away from his neck and dropped him. Once on his hands and knees, Axiom-man quickly got to his feet. The creature stood, a gaping hole in its stomach, and ambled toward him.

A zap of blue energy to the thing's head sent the top of its skull into the dead man just behind it.

A foul shriek forced Axiom-man to spin on his heels. A dead woman with long, red hair latched onto his shoulders with both hands and yanked him toward her, her mouth open, yellow teeth heading straight for his neck. Axiom-man drew his hands in, circled them inside hers. A swift push outward and he released her hold then he grabbed either side of her head, clamped on, then ripped her head clean from her body. Blood bubbled out from her neck like an overflowing toilet and the body dropped.

Another came in from the side. Axiom-man crouched and the thing toppled over his back and flipped over onto the other side. He raised his leg and brought his boot down onto the creature's skull, squishing the bone like stomping on an egg. Brain and bone splattered outward across the floor.

He powered up his eyes and for the second time that day spun in a circle, blasting to bits anything that came near him, giving himself some room. Once done, he saw a row of the dead on the far side of the room not far from the wall that was ablaze. A few of the corpses seemed mesmerized by the flame.

Axiom-man's feet left the ground. He poured on the speed, flew over to them and landed in front of them.

Winding up, Axiom-man shot out his right arm and socked a dead overweight black guy across the cheekbone, sending the fat man sailing through the air and into the wall of fire. Axiom-man picked up another, one hand between the guy's legs, the other over the guy's shoulder, and he hurled him into the flames. The remaining five came for him, hands outstretched, fingers snapping against the air as if already tasting the kill.

Axiom-man kicked one into the fire, blasted the head off another and shoved another into the flames. Two more. Bending down, he grabbed one by the ankles and used its body like a golf club and smacked a female corpse into the fire. Then he threw the young dead man he had by the ankles into the flames as well.

"Burn," he said.

The dead didn't scream, but instead wrestled against the flames, as if the fire itself was something to grapple with.

There were more behind him.

And more lined the railing of the level overlooking the lobby.

The dead rolled over the railing, some jumping to the ground like divers off a pier. Others fell, hit the ground, then got up.

They came for him.

CHAPTER NINE

ADRENALINE COURSING THROUGH him, electrifying every muscle in his body, Axiom-man lunged for the nearest zombie and rolled with it to the floor. Now on top of it, he plowed his fist into the creature's face, crushing its skull, its brains splooshing out through its ears. He jumped off it, spun around, and backfisted another zombie rushing toward him. The dead man's head snapped to the left, the neck broken. It staggered a moment, then tried once more to grab him. Axiom-man came in with a hook and finished the job by permanently removing the thing's head from its body. The zombie dropped.

They came in from all sides, fifteen or twenty of them.

Raw power igniting in his eyes, Axiom-man let the energy build and build, keeping it in until they were closer. Unable to see because of the blinding blue-white light covering his vision, he listened as their dragging footfalls drew nearer. Estimating they were probably now only a few feet away, he let loose, whirled in a circle, and decimated each of the zombies' faces, slicing off the tops of skulls, severing heads or just cleaving skull and face through their centers.

The bodies dropped in a series of thuds.

Strong arms grabbed him from behind. Glancing over his shoulder, filthy blonde hair pressed up against the rear of his neck as a dead woman with a chunk of flesh taken out of her face tried to bite his neck. He elbowed her in the gut, grabbed the arms around him by the forearms, then shot his own arms forward, tearing the woman's limbs from their sockets. He slapped the dismembered appendages to the floor, turned and kicked the woman's head off her neck. Blood spurted from the wound and the body hit the ground.

More coming. Lots more.

Lost in the moment, Axiom-man charged them, got in between a pack of six, and went to work. He kicked the legs out from under one, clocked another in the nose, zapped the face off another and drove his fist into the chest of one more. Getting some room, he took out the remaining two by sending an energy blast through their skulls, ending them.

Another dozen came in from the rear as did at least ten more replacing the six he just dealt with.

ZAP! CRACK! BOOM!

He took out a handful, the energy pulsing from his eyes decimating them.

Two tugged at his cape, hauling him back into a throng of the dead. He lurched forward, trying to get his cape back but instead the material tore and he stumbled forward and had to stop himself from hitting the floor face first with his palms.

"Grrrah!" he shrieked and got to his feet, the remainder of his cape only settling mid back.

He turned to meet them head on. The two that had grabbed his cape each still held an end and fought over it like a couple of children fighting over their favorite toy. Their comrades, not interested in their kins' new find, ambled toward him on dead legs, arms raised, fingers extending and contracting, as if they couldn't gage distance and were already trying to grab onto him.

Side-stepping into the nearest zombie, Axiom-man rammed it with his shoulder then grabbed hold of the creature's arm and threw the monster into its comrade across the way.

One rushed toward him but was quickly stopped with a boot to the gut. The thing doubled over, staggered back, then came at him again still bent at the waist. Just as its down-turned head was about to plow into Axiom-man's stomach, he brought his elbow down into the base of its skull, snapping the bone, while simultaneously drawing his knee up into the creature's face, squishing its skull between elbow and knee.

The groans of the dead erupted throughout the room, each deathly cry stating they'd had enough of being overrun and now it was time to get serious and destroy him.

More of the dead came for him, and more of the dead filled the room, coming out of hallways and out of corners; others toppled over the railing overlooking the carnage and joined in the march.

Axiom-man floated off the ground, the goal to get onto the second level where, from what he could see, only a dozen or so zombies remained. But before his feet cleared their heads he was tugged back down. A mental flashback to the viewing deck at the Forks danced before his eyes where the same thing happened.

Dead fingers clawed and gripped at his costume, tearing bits of it away, others still maintaining their hold as they dragged him to the ground.

SLAM!

His back lit up in numby pain when his shoulder blades struck the floor.

A pair of zombies grabbed him by the ankles. Others dug their hands in by his armpits. Together they began to work at tearing him apart while others leaned over his body, clawing at his guts and legs, jaws snapping, white eyes filled with hate.

Axiom-man jerked and twitched, anything to stop the dead people's fingers from digging in. He only hoped they wouldn't cut him with their bruised and jagged fingernails.

One heavyset woman whose gut was torn open, the intestines hanging over her dirty jeans like a series of loose belts, shoved her way through the creatures, stood over his body for a moment, then jumped on top of him. Some of the dead were able to retract their hands in time, others fell forward when the woman's weight squished their hands and fingers.

She straddled over his middle, her dead white eyes looking into his, unblinking. She leaned back, arms up by her sides, bent at the elbows, then flopped forward, her heavy chest banging into his, ripping the air from his lungs.

Unable to breathe, Axiom-man used the side of his head to smack hers aside as she shoved her face toward his neck. Bone smashed against bone and a dry *whack* spiked from one side of Axiom-man's head to the other.

He needed to breathe.

Blood trickled from the side of her head from where he hit her and she was only dazed for a moment before she came in for another bite.

Need air.

She dug her head in where his jaw met his neck and he could feel her lips rubbing against the material of his suit as she prepared to sink her teeth into him.

Two hard yanks jerked his ankles to either side as the zombies holding him there seemed to now be in co-operation with this fat woman and were positioning his body for the kill.

Arms pinned, legs stuck, lungs screaming for air, only one thought burst clear in Axiom-man's mind: *Over.*

Time slowed.

The fat woman's mouth was open over his neck, her teeth putting pressure against his flesh.

Over.

Her teeth worked their way through the fabric of his uniform and a sharp pain stung his neck when they began to settle in.

Over.

Axiom-man tried tugging his arms and legs toward himself. He couldn't move.

Over.

The teeth dug in. Any moment now she would rip her face away, a piece of his neck along with it, blood and ropey flesh coating her mouth and chin.

Over.

Without thinking, blue light trickled over his line of sight, oozing in at first from the sides until soon it was all he saw.

Tugging at his neck. The flesh about to be torn.

Over.

The light crackling of electric power surfaced in his ears as he braced himself to die or become one of them.

Death.

Blue turned to blue-white.

The woman began to pull her face away. Axiom-man felt the muscles and skin of his neck begin to stretch.

Dead.

The crackling grew louder. The light grew brighter.

Stop.

He lolled his head to the side so it butted up against hers. He couldn't see anything except the power over his eyes.

He let it out and almost immediately the stench of burning hair and flesh and bone rose to meets his nostrils.

Smell. He could smell, though just barely.

His air was returning.

The woman's head shook and tremored as the energy bore into her skull like a drill, spiking into her brain.

Her mouth went lax and her weight settled on top of him.

Axiom-man still couldn't see. The light over his eyes was too bright.

He raised his head from the ground so his chin was resting on his chest then unloaded an all-out energy beam into the fat woman's body, blasting it off of him. Immediately the warmth of blood oozed from his neck and soaked his costume.

Hands and legs still pinned and still unable to see, he rolled his head from side to side against the floor, then forward again down toward his feet, then back and side to side, then forward, then back then side to—the droning calls of the dead blotted out his thoughts, turning his movements to something more subconscious than cognitive.

His hands were released.

Drawing them in toward his chest, the muscles tingly and sluggish, he tried to sit up. Breathing was a bit easier now but it wasn't all there.

Groans and grunts of the walking dead consumed him, their sound permeating every fiber in his body.

The grip around his left ankle lessened so he brought his leg in. Soon after, he was able to do the same with his right.

He still couldn't see.

And he couldn't shut off the power blasting forth from his eyes.

He sat up, careful not to accidentally dismember his own legs with his eye beams.

Blood gushed from the side of his throat.

CHAPTER TEN

"ARRGGHH!" AXIOM-MAN HOWLED as he sat there, a hand to the side of his neck.

The deep throbbing pulse booming against his throat traveled into his brain, making it difficult to concentrate, the warm flow of blood soaking through his glove.

The groans of the dead began to fade behind the veil of blue-white light over his eyes.

Using his right hand, he pressed against the floor, drew his legs in, and slowly got to his feet. His head immediately swooned upon standing. Carefully, he turned in a circle, hoping to take out as many of the creatures as he could.

More groans. More howls.

He rose from the floor, weakly drawing his knees up to his chest to avoid them from being grabbed, and ascended until his back bumped up against the ceiling.

His neck. The pain. The bite.

His racing heart.

How long till I change? What's inside of me?

The energy streamed from his eyes in a continuous flow. Below, the mixed sounds of the floor being torn up and the wails of the dead rose up to meet him. Focusing himself as best as he was able, he mentally envisioned the room behind the blue-white light, hoping that he was facing the right direction and the wall lining the second floor just beyond the railing was somewhat close by.

Slowly, he flew in that direction, hand still clasped to his neck, his other held out before him, his outstretched palm already feeling the wall even though there was no wall there.

He drifted through the air. He began to breathe even easier.

Clink zzzmmmm. Metal cut in two. The railing. He was facing the right direction.

The calls of the dead below began to fade.

His palm touched something hard and smooth and it took several moments to remember what it was he had been reaching for.

The wall.

He was there.

Crchooook crchooom!

Shards of drywall blasted against him; hard tiny pieces stabbed him.

He stopped his flight, dropped his legs and lowered himself to the floor. Before his feet touched the ground, a hot slice of pain shot through his neck and he landed on his knees, his kneecaps igniting in dull pain, one that burst through his legs and lit up his thighs, the echo from impact shaking him all over.

Crchooom!

A rumble then the rain of drywall stopped. His eyebeams must have blown straight through the wall.

The blood. There was too much blood.

"Got to . . . got to turn off . . . my eyes." The words trickled out of his mouth like drool.

Draw it in. Turn it off. Countless times had he summoned his power, let his eyes flood with that glorious blue-white light, wielding the energy like a sword, aiming it wherever he wished. Now the knowledge, even ability, of what to do was gone. He didn't know if he was in survival mode or if his body and mind were so wrapped up in the injury to his neck that he could no longer keep a tight rein on his powers.

"Turn it off," he told himself.

The energy kept flooding outward.

The moans of the dead surfaced on either side of him. There was no way to tell how close they were.

Turn it off.

There was only one option: *shifting.*

Axiom-man took a slow, deep breath through his nose, exhaled and . . .

You're not here. You're at home. You're safe. No costume. No powers. You're nothing. You're worthless. Just Gabriel Garrison. Axiom-man is gone.

The light flickered and a bright flash burst before his eyes before the dark hole in the wall materialized into view.

His neck.

Vision blurred, he glanced over to the hand cradling his throat. The bright blue of his glove was now deep purple, wet and dripping.

In his peripheral on both sides, hazy gray shadows slowly walked toward him. There seemed to be six of them though he couldn't be sure. He tried looking to the nearest bunch to the right, but when he turned his head, his neck immediately objected.

"Need to . . ." . . . *stop the bleeding.* He couldn't leave his hand there but he *needed* it there.

With a trembling right hand, he reached over his left shoulder, past the hand cradling his neck, and began pulling up the remainder of his cape. He did the same to the right side so the bright blue material was bunched up about his neck.

The shadows drew closer, maybe only a few solid paces away.

"On three . . ." he breathed. "One . . . two . . . th—three . . ."

He let go of his neck and with both hands pulled tightly at the bunches of cape on either side and tied it around his neck like an enormous scarf. The wound flashed heat. The flow of blood was unmistakable.

He pulled the knot even tighter despite the pressure it was already putting on his throat. A low, rapid *thwu-thump* pulsed over and over up the sides of his neck, through his jaw and into his head. He could still breathe, but nothing deep. He figured that as long as he had air, he should be okay.

The shadows. A pace away.

Axiom-man got to his feet, eyes still blurry, and turned to face those coming for him.

Mind foggy, he threw a punch at the nearest zombie. His fist rebounded off as if he hit a pillow.

How could— Surely he could have done more damage. Just before he had plowed his fist *into* a zombie's head. He had to be stronger than this. His powers gave him strength. His powers—

His powers.

He forgot he had *shifted* down, had turned them off. He was just as human as the next man.

Snap out of it. Focus.

A dead hand slapped him. His head spun. Panic setting in, fear of not being able to *shift* his powers back on beginning to take him, Axiom-man braced himself for the worst. He shoved the zombie back, his efforts weak.

The zombie pushed him and he stumbled back a few steps.

Others crowded in around him.

Need power.

"Turn. On," he said through gritted teeth. He forced pictures of himself in costume, his powers, the charge from the messenger to the fore of his mind.

Come on.

A flash of blue and a swell of energy bubbled within. Back in business. And good timing, too.

An undead with barely any skin and tissue left covering its skull grabbed him by the shoulder. Axiom-man quickly threw the dead man's arm off himself and socked the thing in the temple. The creature's bone matter must have broken down long ago because the blow cracked the skull like an egg and brain and black blood splashed onto the wall beside it. The thing fell.

Hesitant to use his energy beams in case he couldn't regain control again, Axiom-man turned around and went for one coming in from behind. Without thinking, he head-butted the creature then clamped his fingers to the sides of a dead woman's neck. He squeezed the rotting flesh between his fingers then pulled with a mighty heave, tearing out her throat.

The loss of blood getting to him, he knew he couldn't take out the rest.

The dead drew nearer, backing him against the wall.

The hole he had blasted through it was to his left.

Axiom-man went in, stumbled backward and emerged in darkness, the only light that of the fire consuming the lobby beyond the hole.

He turned and took in the main hall, the rows of seats washed in a sickly orange hue, zombies covering every square foot of the place like flies over road kill.

The funk of the dead made him gag and he had to put a palm to either side of his neck to brace the involuntary jerks as puke rose to the back his throat.

He swallowed it, its sharp lemony taste sending a violent quake through his chest and stomach.

Across the seats and sea of the dead was the pit, then just above that was the stage. The normally-red curtains hung limply from a gold-plated bar several stories up, slightly open, each side with the bottoms ripped and laced with the dark of blood.

The haunting white eyes of the dead that filled the place looked toward him.

The ones he had left on the second floor balcony beyond the hole began to come through.

A flash of purple light snapped on the stage, its violent burst sending a resounding *CRACK* through the air.

Someone was seated on a large ornate chair just behind the partly-opened curtains. He couldn't see who or what, but whatever it was, he could see its eyes.

They glowed with purple light.

Chapter Eleven

REDSAW, WAS AXIOM-MAN'S first thought. But that snap of energy would have been red had it been Redsaw and it wouldn't have come from the eyes either.

Purple light.

There was only one time when an energy zap like that occurred: when the blue power from his eyes clashed with the red from Redsaw's hands.

It didn't make sense.

Before he could think about it further, the zombies from the lobby's second-floor balcony emerged through the hole in the wall, arms outstretched, fingers searching for him.

Axiom-man sidestepped several paces to the left, gaining some distance.

The glow of purple light emanating from who or whatever was on the stage bathed the room, casting faint and eerie illumination on the dead cluttering the seats and filling the aisles.

He took a step closer.

White eyes filled with malice greeted him, the bodies of the dead writhing and bumping into each other like ants swarming over leftovers from a picnic.

Almost as one, they moved toward him, climbing over the seats to get to the aisle lining the back of the second-floor hall where he stood.

The ones who had come through the hole in the wall picked up their pace, growling, jaws open.

There was only one place to go and that was forward, toward the stage, toward that thing with purple eyes.

Axiom-man raised his hands and floated into the air, flying over the mass of the dead below, their vacant stares following him as he did. All seating levels of the hall were filled with the dead. Rows upon rows of them. He paused and hovered over the pit. The zombies stood there, looking up, some with their arms reaching toward the sky as if they could grab him.

He was too high up for them to be of any concern, but there was one down there that drew his attention: a female, one with a decayed face, hollow eyes and grayish-green skin.

"Valerie . . ." he whispered. No, it couldn't be.

The light was too dim to tell for sure, but the creature looked up as if it recognized him.

Not you, Valerie. Anybody but you.

The dead woman below raised her hands like the others, her dead eyes filled with longing, as if reaching out for a hug.

Axiom-man jerked in the air when she left the pit of the dead below and rose up to meet him.

"No . . ." he breathed, hardly able to believe what he was seeing.

She came beside him, kept several feet away, and just studied him. She looked to the stage then back toward him.

Valerie. It was her. She was dead. Her once gorgeous brown hair sat in matted tufts on her head, portions of the hair missing, nothing but dark red scalp remaining. The skin was peeled in places along her jaw and running up along her cheek to just under her eye. A large bite mark had taken a piece of her throat away, enough that even if she wanted to, she probably couldn't talk. Her hands hung limply at her wrists, her once slender and feminine fingers skeletal, the knuckles bony knots.

Heart breaking, tears wetting his eyes, Axiom-man wanted to reach out and hold her, tell her that everything was going to be okay. Gone was the throbbing pain in his neck. Gone were the moans and groans of the throng of the dead below. All that mattered was her.

"What happened?" he asked gently, yearning to know how she got this way, and not just dead but her ability to fly as well.

She just floated there, her body hanging on the air like an old and worn coat off a hook. Her eyes searched his, vacant yet full of memory, memories, it seemed, she knew of but couldn't fully comprehend.

"I'm sorry," he said. "I should have been there for you. I didn't mean to—" The words trailed off and the back of his throat pinched. Then he remembered this wasn't *his* Valerie, but a mere carbon copy from a world that was dead. Yet did it matter? Whoever she once was, she must have been similar if not the same as the Valerie Vaughan he knew back home. The rain that caused this . . . . No one deserved to die like she did. No one deserved to become one of them.

He wanted to speak. To say something. To say *anything.* But the words fled from his mind, nothing left but blank thoughts and deadly heartache.

Quiet groans surrounded him like a cloak. He glanced below. The pit was near empty. So were the seats beyond.

An army of the dead surrounded him, there, in the air.

Valerie floated toward him and lowered her arms until her gray and flaking palms rested on his shoulders. She didn't speak, but only conveyed a sense that his confusion was understandable. That she would be there for him if he would only let her.

She's flying. How—

Numb, emotions crumbling, Axiom-man didn't resist when she gripped his shoulders tight. Didn't pull back when she drew her head next to his, the smell of her rot invading his nostrils.

Valerie leaned in and pressed her dead lips against his cheek and kissed him.

"I'm sorry . . ." he said again.

She pulled her face away from his, her white eyes gazing into his one last time, then opened her mouth wide. She lurched forward, digging into him, her mouth going for the bunch of cape bundled up around the wound on his neck.

Axiom-man reached over her arms, grabbed her by the throat, and tore her off him, hurtling her into the seats below. Tears oozing from the corners of his eyes, he turned to meet the flying crowd of the dead coming for him. Their powers. That would mean . . .

One launched at him, mouth open. Axiom-man slugged the creature in the face, snapping its neck, the head ripping from the body. The thing dropped to the ground. Another came in from behind, grabbing him around the arms. Axiom-man snapped his elbows outward, freeing himself, turned, and sent an energy blast into the thing's face, not caring if he'd lose control of the power again.

Eyes glowing, enough there so he could do some damage yet not too much so he couldn't see, he fired off shot after shot into the flying dead that buzzed around him like a swarm of angry bees.

Thwump. Thwump. Thwump. Their rotted and decayed bodies fell from the sky and plowed into the heads of the zombies below, onto the seats, into the aisles.

Axiom-man flew up and over in an arc, narrowly missing a couple of zombies that had tried to grab him from either side. He blasted a few more from the air and drove his fist into the face of another.

A scraggly old woman locked onto his legs. He reached down, curled his fingers under her jaw, and yanked upward with all his might, ripping her head from her body. The headless body latched onto his legs lost its grip and fell.

More of the dead rose from the seats below, as if they all at once remembered their ability to fly.

Dozens of them sped toward him, knocking into him like a team of football players going for the tackle, plowing him into the hall's roof.

Pain tore through his back, spiked into his neck, and he was sure he felt a fresh gush of blood spurt from the wound. He wanted to reach for the cape tucked up around it to check the damage but just as he raised his arm, one of the dead stopped his hand and pinned it against the ceiling. He tried with his other hand and the same thing happened.

Legs locked, arms stuck, the zombies pressed into him with snapping jaws and ghostly howls.

"AAAAAHHHHH!" Axiom-man screamed and powered up his eyes with nothing but the sheer brilliance of raw blue-white power. He let it build and build, doing his best to restrain it, to fill up as much as he could possibly take and then some. The energy cracked and snapped like lightning around the corners of his eyes, each *SNAP* forcing a wail from the dead, the energy leaking out enough to keep them from biting his face and neck.

More. Make more. Build. BUILD!

The light turned blinding white and—

CRABOOOM!

He moved his head side to side, intense, destructive power pouring from his eyes like a flamethrower, blasting into the heads and bodies of the dead.

The pressure against his torso and limbs began to ease, enough for him to shake his arms and legs loose and fly downward, straight through them. As the power gushed out, his vision began to return and through a bright blue haze he could see them fly toward him, moving in for the kill. Each one that came near was met with an energy blast to the face. And each one that came near fell.

Axiom-man flew toward the stage, landed at its edge, then faced the open hall and summoned his power from within, coating the place in raw energy. Every zombie the beam struck fell from the sky. The walls tore and crumbled when the blast struck them. Large holes punctured the ceiling, letting in the pale gray light from the sky above.

More power.

The howls of the dead echoed throughout the room.

Screaming, Axiom-man let the power take him, joy bursting within with each zombie that fell.

Those things had killed Valerie. Had made *him* kill her.

They had killed Peter.

They had killed that woman outside.

They had taken Tom's kid.

They had torn a chunk out of his neck and, soon, he'd be one of them.

Not without a fight. Not without taking as many down as he could before it was too late.

The shrieks and squeals of the dead grew so loud they merged into a wild drone, one that spiked into Axiom-man's brain and exploded inside his head.

The bodies fell.

The energy poured out.

He spun around, aiming to take out whatever that thing was with purple eyes on the stage.

The moment he did, a flash of purple blasted into his eyes, canceling out the blue, and sent him flying back off the stage and into the pit and into the waiting arms of the few dead that remained there.

The zombies clawed at him, forcing him to the floor.

Grimacing, Axiom-man punched one and sent a blue blast of energy into another. More creatures jumped into the pit, emerging from the smoke of smoldering bodies lining the seats and aisles.

They piled on top of him, kept him down.

He pushed against their weight. There was too many and as strong as he was, he did have his limits.

They tore and ripped at his costume, dry fingernails looking to prepare a nice place for them to sink their teeth into.

Axiom-man powered up his eyes and the second the blue appeared, another *crack* snapped through the air and a flash of purple canceled it out. He tried again.

Crack! Snap!

Purple light stole his power away.

He tried again and again. Each effort was met with awesome purple brilliance.

The zombies pressed in and opened wide. They dug their heads into his gut, his legs, his arms, their teeth already pushing into his skin.

Purple light blasted forth from the stage and shot off the dead who were about to devour him.

Out of the shadows, a lone figure stepped to the edge of stage, stealing Axiom-man's breath away.

CHAPTER TWELVE

THE MAN STOOD there, eyes aglow with ghastly purple. He calmly raised a hand. The zombies around Axiom-man backed away.

It can't be . . . Axiom-man thought, still on his back. He wanted to get up, but the presence of this person before him kept him on the ground. *I don't believe it.*

His mind drifted to Valerie, the dead one from earlier. She was here, part of the chaos that had swept the city. It only made sense that—

The man floated off the edge of the stage and landed at Axiom-man's feet.

The stark realization of death ran from Axiom-man's toes throughout his body, settling into his heart. There was no need for it to go any further. Death was like that. Hit you where it mattered the most.

A dead Axiom-man stood before him, costume torn up and down his limbs, covered in filth, hanging off him like oily rags. Purple energy consumed his eyes. A series of black clouds swirled over and around his body like snakes, never settling, only hovering. The man's mask was torn in two, the light blue side that once ran at an angle across his face gone, revealing the scarred remains of the man beneath. The skin was gray and blotched with open flesh. A portion of the mouth was missing, nothing but yellow teeth and a skeletal jaw line. His hair was murky purple in places, gray in others.

It was the man beneath the mess of flesh that forced Axiom-man to close his eyes. The costume, the powers—they were but a mask. Behind the strength, the flight, the awesome blue energy lurked nothing but a lonely man trying to find his place in the world, to reclaim some sense of self worth after a lifetime of falling short. Here, in this place, he caught a glimpse of what he really was: a man dying beneath a blue suit.

Gabriel Garrison. The name given at birth that was now a mere joke to those who knew him. The name no one knew that was tied to a set of abilities that shook the face of the earth and stood on one side of a cosmic war that he himself was still learning.

Axiom-man opened his eyes.

Despite the man's decaying visage, it was Gabriel who stood before him, the one beneath it all.

Slowly, Axiom-man sat up. The zombies around him didn't move, but instead all in the place looked in seeming awe at the one who had turned them, changed them, given them flight. He was their hero. One of the dead.

Axiom-man managed to get to his feet and put out his arms to either side to steady himself. Gabriel stood before him, unmoving, as if allowing him to try and get things together.

Legs hollow and sapped of strength, Axiom-man eyed his counterpart up and down. The black clouds danced around Gabriel with purpose, their funk the same as that from the night the Doorway of Darkness was opened.

Gabriel's eyes powered down but only a little, the purple remaining. Axiom-man could only assume that this version of himself had gotten distorted not only from becoming one of the dead, but also from the influence of the black cloud and its tie to the red energy that Redsaw wielded.

Could the thing speak?

It only stood there, staring at him, as if he, too, somehow understood what he was seeing.

Axiom-man felt compelled to say something, to ask Gabriel what happened. But he didn't need to. Elise's words from earlier said it all: *Taken. By them.*

Gabriel held his gaze a moment longer then floated up back onto the stage. He touched down and looked to Axiom-man as if to ask him if he was coming. Axiom-man nodded and rose up and landed at his side.

Gabriel led Axiom-man behind the remains of the red curtains, nothing but darkness beyond, the only light that of the little bit coming through the ceiling and the faint purple glow of Gabriel's eyes.

From out of the darkness, a small voice: "Dad?"

Small steps tapped along the stage floor. Gabriel's eyes lit up brighter.

A young boy appeared out of the shadows, racecar jammies and bare feet. The young lad looked just like his father: same round eyes, same blank expression. His brown hair was a mess.

"Axiom-man?" the boy asked. His eyes darted between the two of them, as if deciding which one was the real one.

"Yeah, it's me. Your dad is Tom, right? Tom Marsch?"

The boy nodded.

"What's your name?"

The boy looked to Gabriel, as if seeking permission to give it. Gabriel didn't reply.

The boy shifted on his feet. "P-Payton."

Payton. Payton Marsch. I found you. Finally, I found you. As gently as he could, Axiom-man said, "It's going to be okay, Payton. I'm going to get you out of here."

Payton's brown eyes shot wide, fear gripping his little face.

Gabriel turned to Axiom-man. "My son remains."

The voice. Dark, distorted. But it was his.

Your son? What did—

Death crept up on him again.

Listening to that voice from beyond the grave made his skin crawl and his shoulders tense.

Axiom-man took a step toward Payton. Gabriel shot out his hand, stopping him. Axiom-man didn't care. "You'll be all right. Do you understand me? You'll be all right."

"What about" —Payton raised a small index finger and pointed— "him?"

"You don't worry about that." Axiom-man nodded toward the shadows at the back of the stage. "Is it safe back there? Are there any . . . any monsters?"

Payton shook his head.

"I want you to go back there and stay there till I come get you. Don't come out. No matter what happens, don't come out. Stay there."

The boy nodded then looked to Gabriel as if asking if this was all right.

Gabriel pressed his palm against Axiom-man's chest. The dead man's very touch permeated through the remains of the fabric of his costume and seeped into his skin. His neck ached, pounded and his head grew dizzy. His heartbeat jumped into a gallop.

"My son remains," Gabriel said.

Chapter Thirteen

"Your son," Axiom-man said. "He's not your son."

"Payton is mine," Gabriel replied. "There's no one else in the world that I love more."

Love. Axiom-man hadn't expected the man to say it. Hadn't expected him to be capable of it. Yet there was one thing that remained beyond death and it was love.

But there was no way to understand this. How could this . . . thing . . . offer love? How could it know the difference between true, living, breathing love and . . . and whatever this was, something distorted, mixed and altered?

"You speak of love," Axiom-man said. "What about Valerie? If you're anything like me, you know that she is the one that you'd give anything for, the one you would have kept alive."

Gabriel's eyes exploded in bright purple and a blinding pulse of energy sped forth, zapping Axiom-man in the chest and hurtling him through the air across the stage, his body slamming into the side wall. He went limp on impact and he fell to the ground.

"You don't know anything about her. She was . . . she was there!" Gabriel said and pointed out to the remaining zombies in the hall. There was a pause before he lowered his hand. "She wanted to . . . to join me. To be like me. I obeyed, granted her eternal life. Gave her freedom. She flew." He walked over to Axiom-man, grabbed him by the collar of his uniform, and lifted him off the ground so his feet dangled in the air. "And you killed her."

Axiom-man so badly wanted to take Gabriel down, to end this madness and somehow get home. But not yet. There was something happening here, something profound, a glimpse into a side of him he didn't know existed. If he survived this, he needed this knowledge. Needed to improve himself so he could better serve his city and its people.

"That wasn't Valerie," Axiom-man said. "She might have been yours, but she wasn't mine."

Gabriel threw Axiom-man to the floor. Axiom-man rolled, flowing with the momentum, the impact barely noticeable everywhere else except for his neck. Lightheadedness crept in and the stage tipped beneath him like the deck of ship on a rolling sea. Something was . . . different. He couldn't place it, but something had changed within. The strength began to seep from his body like water being wrung out from a sponge.

"I did what I thought was right. What *you* thought was right," Gabriel said.

So he does understand, Axiom-man thought. *He knows I'm him. Or a version of him, anyway. He doesn't seem to . . . seem to think it's important. If he does, he's not showing it. Perhaps dying has changed his outlook on things, altered his perspective.*

"Why Payton?" Axiom-man said. *Keep him talking. Figure out what's going on with you.* He pressed his palms against the floor and pushed himself up onto his knees.

The black clouds erupted around Gabriel's body, each growing bigger, thicker, as if an emotional response to the question. What was strange was that they didn't change when he had brought up Valerie. Only the boy.

"This world is dead," Gabriel said. He put a hand to his chest. "*I'm* dead. The pulse . . . . There is no pulse. There is no warmth. There's . . ." He didn't finish.

Axiom-man got to his feet. The side of his neck throbbed but it didn't feel as if any more blood was oozing out of the wound. He hoped that was the case and that the wound hadn't paralyzed the surrounding nerves so bad he wasn't feeling anything.

"I'm . . ." Axiom-man put a palm to the side of his neck and stumbled a step to the side. "I'm taking the boy."

"No," Gabriel said. "My son remains. He's drunk of the clouds. He'll be my son and I'll be his father."

The dead man strode over to Axiom-man; the stink of the clouds mixed with the funk of death made his stomach swirl.

"He'll heal me," Gabriel said.

"You can't do this. You can't possibly think that a boy—a boy who doesn't belong here—will restore you." The next words out of his mouth broke his heart. "You're beyond saving."

"No, my friend. It is you who are beyond saving. It is you who will join us today. You will guide Payton at my side. We can save the world."

*He's right. We need Payton to save us. We need to overcome what has happened and override the storm. We need to make the world like us if we cannot change it back. We—*He snapped himself out of his thoughts. He didn't know where they came from.

The change. He was turning.

His throat was dry; a yearning for something rich and deep, thick and red tickled the back of his throat. Made his stomach ache. And something more. Something *thicker.*

Something filled with life. A chance to touch something he was losing.

Himself.

"Oh no . . ." Axiom-man breathed, his voice shaky. His hands began to tremble and the muscles in his legs began to give way. A rush of cool swept over his body, causing the hairs on his arms, legs and neck to stand on end.

He was dying.

"Let it take you. You are too far gone to bring us back. But Payton . . . he can save us," Gabriel said.

"Why . . . why him?" Axiom-man asked.

"You know why. You know his father. Tom, the one you always felt bad for. The one ignored at work. The one you related to on a level you're only now beginning to understand. To use his son as a means to save an entire world—think of the pride! The relief! The value!" Gabriel chuckled, low and offbeat.

"Why not Tom?"

"Because it wouldn't be pure. He's too old, too jaded. Payton is new."

"Are you saying that somehow Payton's . . . thoughts . . . would transfer to . . ." He wasn't sure what he was asking. He only kind of knew what Gabriel was driving at.

"His ideals, his admiration for you—for us—would merge with us and bring us back to the light."

The light.

The light was beginning to fade. Axiom-man didn't know when it happened but he was on his knees again.

He only hoped that the darkness closing in around his eyes wouldn't be all he'd see when he awoke.

———

"Take my hand," Gabriel said somewhere off in the shadows.

"No," Payton said, his voice barely a whisper.

Axiom-man opened his eyes. He was still on his knees but he was bent at the waist, face pressed against the floor. Hunger pains streaked through his stomach but the thought of food repulsed him. But meat. Raw meat. Oh yeah. That was it.

Am I . . . is it . . . He was still cold. He reached under himself and touched his chest. His heart was still beating but only faintly. He hadn't even noticed it slow down. The muscles in his body were sluggish and he knew that the blood wasn't getting to them as well as it used to anymore.

"Stand up, Payton," Gabriel said. "Feel this cloud."

"Help! Axiom-man, help!"

Whack!

The boy yelped and was silent.

Head pounding, Axiom-man squeezed his eyes shut, absorbed the pain, and forced himself to his feet.

The stage was dark toward the back, the front half lit up by the orange glow from the fire that had made its way through from the lobby into the main hall. The orange light was strong enough to mute out nearly all of the gray light coming in through the holes in the ceiling now.

Careful with his steps, he slowly made his way toward the back of the stage to where he thought he had heard Gabriel's and Payton's voices.

If he was to die, it was going to be today.

But not without a fight.

CHAPTER FOURTEEN

IT GREW DARKER and darker and by the time Axiom-man emerged on the other side of another curtain, it was difficult to see much of anything. The only light came in from the floor-to-ceiling "window" created by either side of the curtain, everything cast in a faint orange hue. The sharp smell of smoke from the burning concert hall mixed with the putrid stench of the dead. The air was already misty from the smoke and Axiom-man's eyes watered.

Gabriel and Payton were silent.

His leg bumped into something with a dull metallic *clang*. He put a palm down and felt around, his fingers running along what felt like an old, brass bed frame. To his right stood an out-of-commission antique lamp. To his left a dresser with a filthy mirror on top. His mind immediately flashed back to Payton's bedroom the night the boy was stolen. Back to the present, he walked around the bedroom set and had to quickly get out of the way of a clothes rack loaded with fifteenth century clothing, the rack at first seeming to have been thrown in his path. He realized it was just his mind playing tricks on him and the thing had been stationary the whole time.

So . . . so sluggish, he thought. Concentrating on the here and now was getting increasingly harder by the second. The hunger pains wracking his stomach only made matters worse. He wanted to find the boy, if only to feed. "Stop it!" he said louder than he meant to. He froze in his tracks, thinking maybe Gabriel heard him and now knew his whereabouts.

Axiom-man walked on, heading toward where he thought the back of the stage was, but with having to weave his way around the multitude of props and costumes and layers and layers of painted canvas backdrops, he wasn't entirely sure he was moving in the right direction at all.

He stopped. Listened. Waited.

Silence.

The shrieks of the dead burning from beyond the curtains behind him made his insides lock, not out of fear or panic but out of a twisted instinctive concern for his fellow man. His fellow *dead* man.

"It's over," he breathed. "You're changing. Too far gone."

Pressure built up in his head, a million blank thoughts racing through, the stress of losing himself sending off bells of panic throughout his body. His slowly-beating heart picked up its pace in response. Finally, a good sign that he wasn't completely gone.

He kept moving forward. One step. Two. Hand outstretched before him, the need to cradle the wound on his neck no longer present but now, every time it crossed his mind, a nuisance.

Bump. His gloved hand found the rear wall.

Barely able to see much of anything, he let a faint film of blue light cover his eyes to provide subtle illumination. The stage opened up at the left and the right, opening into areas he could only assume were once used for performers to enter and exit the stage.

No Gabriel. No Payton.

Which way? he wondered. Each one was as good as the other.

He was already slightly facing the right so decided to go in that direction. One step. Two. His feet heavy, as if filled with sand.

He stumbled a step, his legs folding beneath him. Just before his knees crashed against the floor, he kicked on his flight and stopped his body from tumbling forward. He hovered backward and planted his feet down, counting to ten to steady himself.

"Keep moving," he told himself, not meaning to say so out loud. He clamped his mouth shut, the gesture enough to amplify the pressure in his brain. It felt like his head was going to explode at any moment.

Was this what happened when you died? That all remaining life found its way into your head, one last effort to think every thought you might have thought before you died? One last chance to ponder the meaning of life and existence before checking out? One last chance for reflection on accomplishment and regret? He wasn't quite there yet though he expected the moment to arise any second now.

God, if You're up there, I could really use a hand right now. The prayer came out of nowhere but seemed a fitting thing to think. Most people said some sort of prayer before they died. Life seemed to begin and end with religion.

The small hall to the right of the stage drew nearer.

One step. Two.

He had to put his hand against the back wall to keep himself steady and it was becoming increasingly harder to keep his head upright and not stare at his boots.

His uniform hung in tatters on his body, looking not all that dissimilar from the costume adorning Gabriel's rotting frame.

Soon he would be just like him.

Soon he would be with Payton.

He only hoped he wouldn't hurt the boy and if that moment came, it would be because he lost control and couldn't help himself.

One step. Two.

He could tell his exposed skin was already losing color even here in the shadows.

One step. Tw—

Something hot and wet fell from above, dripping onto the exposed skin of his forearm. At first he thought it might have been his own sweat running off his head, which was now leaning against the wall, his left forearm not far under it. But when it happened again, he paused to take a look. Instead of clear liquid, through the blue haze covering his eyes, there was a splash of purple.

Blood. Red blood. Not black and oily like that of the creatures.

He looked up.

Between the rafters several stories above the stage was the faint outline of humanoid shapes.

He cast his gaze to the floor, hoping that whatever was up there hadn't seen him looking up.

The thoughts came all at once and for a moment he forgot what it was he was supposed to be thinking about.

Another warm drop splashed against his arm. Then another.

"Payton . . ." he whispered.

They were up there. The shadows were theirs.

He needed to get to them and the only way he might be able to do it unnoticed was to extinguish the blue glow from his eyes and use the shadows to his advantage. But if he did that, he'd hardly be able to see at all.

Just get up there, grab the boy, fly to the front of the stage, between the curtains and out the . . . out the . . . He didn't know anymore. Much of what went on prior to his being here in the dark was fading from memory.

So thirsty.

As if on autopilot, he brought his left forearm to his mouth and licked the blood off it. He could no longer remember what blood was supposed to taste like and he didn't care. This . . . this was amazing. Sweet like honey. Warm like tea.

"Oh no . . ." He licked his lips and winced for further indulging himself in the taste of blood. His heart didn't quicken but instead barely thumped at all.

"I'm sorry," he whispered.

He looked up again. The humanoid shapes looked different and he wasn't sure if they had moved or if it was only his imagination.

He was going to die today, he knew.

He just hoped it would be after the boy was safe.

If Payton wasn't dead already.

CHAPTER FIFTEEN

THE BLOOD HADN'T quenched Axiom-man's thirst nor calmed the aches in his stomach. No matter. It was all going to be over soon anyway. He swallowed the cotton ball at the back of his throat and cut the power from his eyes.

All went black and it took him a moment to remember that was what he wanted.

Use the wall as a guide. Do it quick, he thought.

He pressed his chest against the wall, reached up his hands, laying his palms flat against its surface. He couldn't feel its coolness through his gloves anymore unlike before. Fingers already turning numb, knowing the rest of his body would soon follow, Axiom-man rose off the floor and floated as quickly as he could toward the rafters above.

It took a long time to reach the top and there was another delayed reaction on his part when it came time to stop his ascent once his fingertips touched the roof. He set his feet down on the nearest rafter, turned, and searched for Gabriel and Payton.

Dark beams ran horizontal straight out in front of him, connecting with a short, two-foot wall that rimmed the front of the stage. There was the main curtain, hanging off its gold-plated bar. Other beams crisscrossed off the horizontal ones like symmetrical spider webs.

The smell of smoke wasn't as thick up here. But another smell was: rotten fish mixed with garbage.

The stench of the black clouds.

He was close.

Axiom-man listened intently for Payton: a cry, a whimper, something to signal the boy was still alive.

Two purple dots lit up down one of the beams to the left, about twenty feet away. It was Gabriel. The dead man seemed to search the dark before the dots aimed down and fixed their attention on something else.

He didn't see you. He didn't see you. He didn't see you. He didn't see you. Axiom-man pressed his palms against either side of his head, silencing the repeating thought, control over his mind slipping by the second.

He waited in the shadows, formulating a plan. Nothing fancy, just something to get the job done.

When Gabriel's glowing purple eyes looked up again, Axiom-man launched off the rafter and flew straight for him, tempted to blast Gabriel from his place.

Not yet. Don't fire up your . . . He didn't know the word he was looking for.

No more than one foot away from Gabriel and a flash of purple light shot forth from the dead man's eyes, striking Axiom-man in the top of the chest. Axiom-man tumbled back through the air and crashed into a set of rafters not far beyond, grabbing hold of one of the beams just as he slid off its side.

"You're too late!" Gabriel called from the darkness.

"Now he knows I'm here," Axiom-man said and swung off the beam and dove into the air, heading straight for Gabriel.

When he was almost upon him, he let blue light fill his eyes. Immediately a purple beam shot toward him. Expecting it, Axiom-man veered to the left, flew past

Gabriel, reveling in the sudden surge of *awareness* that seemed to come upon him. He just hoped it would last.

He circled around Gabriel and came in from the rear.

Gabriel was hunched over Payton, who lay prone across his lap, the black clouds dancing around the boy like spirits over a tombstone.

Axiom-man fired off a shot. Gabriel met it with a beam of his own and the two energy blasts collided in mid air in a brilliant flash and deafening *CRACK!*

Flying underneath the beam where Gabriel was, Axiom-man got some distance, spun around mid air, then headed for him, sending off another blast of raw power, this one meant to do damage.

Gabriel blocked the blast with a beam of his own.

Axiom-man tried again. Gabriel countered.

Payton lay still.

"Leave us!" Gabriel shouted.

"No!"

Axiom-man brought his fists together before him, his fingers having trouble curling into his palms. *Who cares? Just push him.* He flew toward Gabriel with the intention of slamming into him. Instead, a zap of purple sliced through the air, its hot sting ripping along the tops of Axiom-man's forearms, burning the skin and removing the layer of costume from his shoulders.

Another burst of energy from Gabriel's eyes sent him hurtling through the air into another patch of rafters, the small of his back hitting the sharp corner of one of the beams. He tumbled over it, fell several feet toward the stage before kicking on his flight and zooming through the air back at his enemy.

He sent off a shot of his own. The blue beam streaked through the air; Gabriel extinguished it with a blast of his own.

"We're at a critical juncture. The boy's been taken by the—" Gabriel started but silenced as he sent off another energy beam to counter another from Axiom-man.

"Arrgh!" Frustration swelled in Axiom-man's gut, voiding the sharp hunger pains. For a moment, his mind made note that he was thirsty then the next moment he shoved the thought away.

Zap!

Crack!

Boom!

Blue and purple lights lit up the top of the stage, blasting this way and that as Gabriel countered every move Axiom-man made. Some shot through the beams, weakening them, shards of dark wood falling to the stage below.

Axiom-man smiled.

He came at Gabriel again, his eyes filled with brilliant blue light. Immediately Gabriel's purple eyes locked onto him, powering up, as if waiting to void yet another blue blast. Axiom-man headed straight toward him and when he was only a few feet away, he quickly changed his course, cut the power from his eyes, and plowed into the beam not far from where Gabriel sat.

"Ah!" Gabriel shouted, the beam creaking as it suddenly dropped a few feet on its broken side. Gabriel and Payton slid along it, gravity already taking its toll.

Axiom-man circled around and crashed through the beam where it was still attached along its flank.

The beam fell from the rafters, taking Gabriel and Payton along with it.

Gabriel's body left the beam as he began to fly.

Payton fell.

Axiom-man swooped in, caught the boy in his arms, and brought him to the ground. His feet folded beneath him when he went to land, spraining both his ankles. Falling forward, Axiom-man tossed the boy out in front of him. Payton's little body rolled along the ground and settled against a stack of cardboard boxes which teetered on impact. Only one fell, its corner landing in front of Payton's face.

Breathing a sigh of relief, Axiom-man went to stand. The sharp and hot pain in his ankles didn't let him. On his knees, he tried again but immediately went down.

Gabriel flew toward him, eyes ablaze in purple light.

CHAPTER SIXTEEN

ADRENALINE PUMPING THROUGH him, Axiom-man punched on his flight, rose off the floor, taking the pressure off his ankles. He righted himself, his feet hovering a scant few centimeters from the ground.

Don't touch down, he thought, ankles throbbing.

Gabriel sped in for the kill.

Axiom-man flew straight up, Gabriel zipping by underneath him. Axiom-man turned in the air, readying a blast that would end this evil mirror image of himself once and for all. Eyes coated in blue light, he was about to let loose when he lost sight of Gabriel. He searched the ground below. There! To the side. He shot off the blast. Gabriel met it with one of his own. The two beams collided in mid air, their merging sending off a crack of thunder that caused the whole place to shake.

It took a moment for the light to dim enough so Axiom-man could see. Just as he was able to, a pair of strong hands gripped him by the ankles, sending a sharp wave of pain up his shins, through his knees and into his thighs. The room spun and the next thing he knew he was in the air. His back rammed into something flat and soft, like being plowed into a slab of towels on a clothesline. He fell to the ground. Whistling from above. A huge blanket of canvas folded over top of him, the high cylindrical beam that had held it in place coming down with it. Axiom-man curled into the canvas's fold, the canvas covering him as the beam crashed down somewhere behind him.

Rrrrrrppppp.

Strong fingers grabbed him from behind, yanked him out from under the canvas and threw him into the back wall. He landed against it with a body-shattering *thwack!*

Gabriel stood before him and Axiom-man wondered if the dead man's flesh was edible.

Just a taste, he thought. A whisper filled his head, a voice distant and dark, speaking in a language he didn't understand, the only notion to obey it once the metamorphosis was complete and he was one of the dead.

"Quiet!" Axiom-man shouted, dizziness suddenly taking him. He tipped over onto his side.

Gabriel marched over to him. "Don't fight it. It'll only make it worse."

Was Gabriel right? Should he just give in?

So tired. His body felt full of lead weight. All he would have to do was close his eyes and he'd drift away only to awake in another form, one, judging by Gabriel's performance, more powerful than anything he imagined.

I love you, Valerie. The thought came out of nowhere, but if he was going to think one thought before he died, that would have been it. She was out there, *his* Valerie, somewhere, in another world. If he died here, he would never see her again. She cared about him, he knew. Cared about both Axiom-man and, he thought, him, as Gabriel Garrison, even though the latter was not what he hoped for himself. Still, she cared about him.

Yet this Gabriel . . . . If the man was able to cross between worlds and kidnap a young boy, what would stop him from one day coming through the portal and slowly but surely transforming the planet into an undead world?

But he was trying to save himself, to become human again, Axiom-man thought. *What if he gave up? What if he couldn't do it? The black cloud won't help him. He's forgotten that. The cloud gave Redsaw his power and Redsaw is the one we're—I'm— supposed to stand against. Gabriel . . .*

The dead man took hold of his neck and drew him to his feet. Axiom-man kept his flight on and his heels hit a thick pillow of air when Gabriel tried to plant Axiom-man's feet down. The dead man's brow furrowed at the obstruction then lightened, as if he didn't care.

Haunting purple eyes glowed bright.

This was it.

It was done.

"Join us," Gabriel said. "Your body is already too far gone that this won't even hurt." He tightened his grip on Axiom-man's neck, cutting off the air. "Hold still."

I love you, Valerie. Axiom-man braced himself.

He raised his arms, fighting against the invisible pull that insisted on keeping them at his sides.

Gabriel's eyes glowed hot and bright, the purple energy crackling like sparklers around his sockets.

Brighter and brighter.

He can't see me, Axiom-man thought and drew his arms around Gabriel's as fast as he could.

Bracing himself for an onslaught of pain, he ground his teeth together and clamped his hands on either side of Gabriel's head, digging his thumbs into the dead man's eye sockets, blinding electric pain shooting through his hands and into his arms, forcing the bones beneath his muscles to ache so bad it felt like someone had taken a wooden baseball bat across his forearms.

Gabriel shrieked.

Muscles beginning to lock, Axiom-man dug his thumbs in further, squishing Gabriel's eyes. Murky white mush oozed from the sides of the eye sockets and trickled down Gabriel's face. Holding on as tight as he could, Axiom-man snapped his hands outward and ripped Gabriel's eyes from his face, decimating the bone just beside the man's temples. The purple light ceased and black blood and shards of bone sprayed out as Axiom-man tore his hands away.

A pair of sledgehammers drove into Axiom-man's chest, digging him into the wall. Gabriel shoved himself off Axiom-man's body and landed back first on the ground, hands covering his face, wailing.

About to pounce on top of him and finish it once and for all, Payton whimpered off to the side.

"Help. Please help," the boy called.

Axiom-man looked in his direction. "I can't go over there," he breathed. If he did, he knew he'd kill the boy. The mere thought of sinking his teeth into the boy's flesh was sheer ecstasy. He could only imagine the euphoria he'd feel if he actually did it.

He looked back to where Gabriel lay. Gabriel was gone.

Payton shrieked off to the side. "Axiom-man, help!"

"I'm coming," he said, heart aching at what might happen once he arrived.

He was there in no time.

Cowering up against the side wall, Payton had his knees drawn up to his chest, face in his hands. Gabriel stumbled toward him, feeling his way over to the boy.

The black clouds erupted around him, expanding and retracting like a set of lungs.

"Payton, no!" Axiom-man screamed and flew toward Gabriel, grabbing him at the waist. He steered Gabriel away and the two crashed into a hat rack and a tall, oval upright wooden-framed mirror.

The mirror shattered, a few of the shards puncturing Axiom-man's flesh along his arms. His skin and tissue were so far gone they felt like mere pinpricks and nothing more.

The black clouds around Gabriel's body seethed. Axiom-man's arms fell into him, as if the man's body wasn't even there but only a strange mist, his hands buried into separate black clouds. A cold mist permeated his palm on the other side of one of the clouds, what felt like hot water on the other.

Portals.

Gabriel knocked Axiom-man off him with flailing arms and legs. Axiom-man fell back near Gabriel's feet, crashing into a set of wig stands that had been on the ground near the mirror.

The dead man stood, body swaying, balance gone.

Something hard rolled up against Axiom-man's side. The hatrack. He grabbed it, brought it across his middle and snapped it in two.

Gabriel turned to meet him. Axiom-man floated into the air and drove the sharp broken end of the rack's pole into his adversary. The tip of the pole plowed into a black cloud across Gabriel's chest. Gabriel moved forward along the pole, the black cloud swallowing the thing inch by inch. Someone screamed from beyond the dark of the hole.

Axiom-man yanked it out. The rear of the pole butted up against another clothes rack, its end getting caught in the fabric so he couldn't discard it. Gabriel felt along the pole, knocked it aside, and latched onto Axiom-man's shoulders with both hands. The dead man's mouth opened wide, long yellow teeth that appeared to have grown and been filed to sharp points bearing down on him.

Axiom-man shot out his hands, one clamping on to the top of Gabriel's head, the other under the jaw. He tried to close Gabriel's mouth but the man was too strong, even in the jaw, and was able to keep his mouth open.

The mouth drew closer, the gray tongue inside flopping around like a dead fish, already tasting Axiom-man's flesh.

Growling, Gabriel jerked his body forward and took Axiom-man down. The back of Axiom-man's head smacked against the ground and a burst of black stars danced across his vision.

Payton shrieked off to the side.

"Stay . . . there . . ." Axiom-man managed. Barely.

Gabriel's fingers clawed at the bunched up cape around Axiom-man's neck, the man's nose sniffing in loud breaths, sensing the wound.

His face drew closer. Axiom-man couldn't press it away.

Blue light flooded his eyes, building and building. He steered Gabriel's face as much to the side as he could, hoping to . . .

Crackjoooommmm.

The blue energy beam sliced into Gabriel's neck, sending out a spray of syrupy black strings, the flesh tearing, burning. Bubbled gasps squeaked from Gabriel's throat as did blobs of goopy black liquid. The blue beam kept cutting, cutting, cutting. Gore and flesh sprayed out and fell down like a sloppy rain, splashing onto Axiom-man's face and hands. He pressed against Gabriel's face, keeping the teeth away.

He let the energy pour out of his eyes, gush forth, as he strained against Gabriel forcing his teeth toward his neck.

So much pressure. So much strain.

And then release when Gabriel's head pulled away from his neck.

The dead man's body tipped to the side.

The creature's head was still in his hands. Axiom-man tossed it away, not caring where it landed.

Payton was in hysterics. "Axiom-man! Dad! Help! Home! Teddy! Dad!"

Axiom-man lay there.

The thirst took him.

The hunger roared.

Chapter Seventeen

Axiom-man got to his feet and stormed over to Payton, grunting each step of the way. He could almost see himself stumbling toward the boy like a drunk looking for his next fix, there, somewhere outside himself. The pain in his ankles was gone. His heart barely beat. Mind empty, he let the whispers of the night fill his brain, their words rhythmic and soothing, encouraging him to eat his fill.

The boy peeked out from behind his hands, his little tear-stained eyes no longer of any consequence; they did not produce any sense of compassion.

"Something has me, Axiom-man," the boy said. "I feel funny inside."

Mouth slack, Axiom-man licked the inside of his mask, his tongue recoiling at the dry taste of the fabric yet thrilling at the prospect of the fresh flesh about to settle between his teeth.

He reached up and tore the bottom of his mask away. Drool spilled from the corners of his lips and rolled down his chin.

So thirsty. So hungry.

Soon. Soon he would be filled.

Payton gazed up at him with hopeful eyes then his gaze quickly turned to fear as Axiom-man reached down and picked the kid up from underneath his arms. The boy hung limply before him.

"Axiom-man?" Payton asked. "There's . . ."

Axiom-man's mouth opened wide on its own accord and he drew the boy in. Yes. There. That soft spot underneath the jaw. The kid's veins glowed beneath his skin, the young lad's smell intoxicating. Axiom-man leaned in and put his teeth to the boy's throat.

Payton spoke, his voice small, faded, somewhere beyond the whispers. "You were supposed to save me."

Axiom-man's teeth settled onto the skin, his mouth yearning to clamp down and tear a bite out of him.

But he couldn't. The boy just hung there, unmoving, not struggling. He was letting him do this.

Why?

"I thought we were friends?" Payton said.

Axiom-man pulled his mouth away and held the boy at arms length. When he spoke, his voice was low, dark. "Friends?"

Tears spilled from the corners of the boy's eyes. "I thought you were supposed to take me home?"

Home. Winnipeg. Home. "This is home."

"No, the other home. The one where my dad is."

"Dad?"

"My dad Tom. Take me home, Axiom-man. Take me home."

His mouth was dry, his throat parched. His stomach rumbled and his muscles felt strangely weak.

He set the boy down.

"We can't get home, Pay—" He didn't know how the rest of it went.

"I want to go home."

Axiom-man turned away and dragged his feet along the floor as he got some distance from the boy. "There's no turning back," he said.

Flames rushed in from behind the curtain; the props, clothes and wooden stands lit up. The canvas backdrops went ablaze and the roar of fire and rush of smoke filled the area.

Axiom-man turned around.

The boy looked toward the side of the stage. "We go home together." And held out his hand to him.

He wanted to take it, but knew if he did, the kid would die. He would die, too. It was happening now. He fell to his knees, barely able to see and barely able to really understand what was going on at all other than it was all wrong and he had to do something but he just didn't know what.

The kid came over to him—he couldn't remember the boy's name anymore—and put a hand on his shoulder. "You were supposed to save me."

Axiom-man glanced about the stage. Gabriel's body lay there, dead, blood still spilling from his neck. Axiom-man wanted to go over and lap it up but he knew it wouldn't do any good. Dead blood wasn't the same as . . . as—

He grabbed Payton about the waist and threw him on top of Gabriel's body.

Screaming, Payton tried to scramble off the corpse but the black cloud slowly rising from the body held onto him and began sucking him in.

"You were supposed to save me! You were supposed to take me home!" Payton shrieked.

Axiom-man forced a faint smile. "Then go."

The black cloud swallowed the boy.

Axiom-man tipped forward and used his forearms to brace his fall. Instead, he collapsed on top of them, face down.

Soon the flames would engulf him and it would all finally be over.

I love you, Valerie. He imagined her back home, sitting at her desk at the Owen Tower office fielding calls and sorting emails, completely oblivious that he was here, in another world, a few moments away from death and, eventually, a bizarre resurrection. He would never get to tell her who he really was or how he truly felt. He would never get to find out why she treated him poorly as Gabriel Garrison and why she seemed to adore him as Axiom-man.

She'd never get to know the real him, the man who was between his two sides, a combination of both but a separate man all the same.

"I want to go home," he groaned.

He crawled toward Gabriel's body.

A rush of flame brewed up to meet him.

EPILOGUE

THE SMOKE SETTLED around him, hovering along the dark floor like a mist above a lake. Axiom-man closed his eyes against its sting, covered his head and waited for the flames to take him. Instead . . . nothing. The air was cool, quiet. All except for—

"Axiom-man?"

A voice. So small, so concerned.

He raised his head from his arms. Payton stood before him.

He knew the boy's name.

What had hap—

He slid back onto his knees and set his palms on his thighs. His ankles throbbed. The stage was empty, dark.

Gabriel's body was gone.

"Are you okay?" Payton asked, bending only slightly at the waist so they were eye level.

"I'm . . . I'm . . ." He reached up and felt the side of his neck. The flesh was puckered, but not bleeding. His head was clear.

He wasn't thirsty. Wasn't hungry.

Hands shaking, he got to his feet, pain piercing his ankles. He rose a few centimeters above the floor and floated toward the front of the stage. The curtain was intact. He parted it with his fingers and stepped out onto the stage proper and faced the hall. Rows and rows of seats, all levels, sat empty. The holes in the ceiling were gone.

Payton came out from the curtain behind him and stood at his side.

"I want to go home," he said.

———

Axiom-man flew the boy home, leaving the hall and the shrill sound of it security alarm behind them.

The soft glow of the early morning sun bathed the city in yellow. Below, cars lined the roadways, early morning travelers on their way to work. Axiom-man cringed on the inside knowing that that was where he was supposed to be either already or very soon. But right now, it didn't matter. Payton was safe. So was he. He just hoped this was *his* Winnipeg and not another carbon copy of the city he loved.

More time had passed in that other world. Not as much here. That black cloud seemed to have some sort of hold over Time, too.

He landed on the front steps to the Marsch residence and set the boy down.

Without even thanking him, Payton opened the door and ran inside, his tiny feet thudding along the wooden flooring straight for the hall.

"Dad! Dad! Dad!" he called.

Axiom-man followed behind.

"Payton!" Tom shouted from down the hallway, presumably from the boy's bedroom. Tom's wails and tear-soaked cries filled the house.

A couple of officers emerged from the kitchen and ran toward the bedroom.

Axiom-man passed by the front room to join them when an all too familiar voice came from the sofa across from the window.

"Welcome back." It was Gunn.

Axiom-man clenched his fists. This was one guy he didn't want to deal with right now.

Gunn rose off the sofa and stepped toward him. The man's eyes were rimmed purple. The guy had obviously been awake all night. "Where was he?" He eyed Axiom-man up and down and only now seemed to realize his costume was shredded. "You look terrible."

There was nothing he could say. Nothing Jack would believe. "I brought him home," Axiom-man said.

———

Jack poked and prodded as to where Axiom-man had found the boy. Axiom-man remained silent the whole time and let Payton do all the talking. Each time the kid mentioned the word "zombie" all the adults in the room looked to Axiom-man for verification. Axiom-man had hoped his appearance would tell it all, that he wouldn't have gotten as banged up and ripped up as he did had the boy been in the hands of mere humans. Instead, he just remained there, hovering slightly to keep the pressure off his ankles, arms crossed, expressionless.

Now, flying home, thinking of excuses he could tell a doctor and his boss without overtly lying, Axiom-man thought back to Gabriel, the one who had died in that world beyond. Here, in this world, he was a man given so much power—a gift—which the messenger told him he had used wisely. He knew his charge. Knew what he was up against and the threat that Redsaw posed. But over there, in that other place, Gabriel had fallen and went beyond redemption. He had taken the boy, one last attempt to regain his humanity. Axiom-man shuddered at the thought that he would have done the same.

He only prayed he wouldn't have slipped like Gabriel had and become a creature of death, not just outwardly, but inwardly as well.

Power was a tricky thing. Too many people had used it for evil even though they meant well initially.

It had happened to Redsaw.

It could happen to him.

He touched the side of his neck. The wound didn't hurt. Whatever had infected him must have been filtered out when he and Payton crossed through the portal. He just hoped that the darkness that had nearly taken him was gone for good.

———

His father at the edge of his bed, Payton was tucked in beneath the blankets. It had taken the police a couple more hours since Axiom-man left before they finally left the house as well.

"I almost lost you today, son," his dad said.

"I know. But Axiom-man saved me."

His dad leaned forward and hugged him. "I love you."

"I love you, too, Dad."

When his father released him, tears wet the man's eyes. Payton couldn't help but tear up himself.

The two looked at each other for a long time before his dad stood from the bed and slowly made his way toward the bedroom door.

"Do you want the light on or off?" his father asked.

Payton glanced toward the closet door. It was closed. "Are you sure there's nothing in there?"

His father smiled. "It's all cleaned up but let me check one more time, okay?" He went over, opened the door, peered in and searched side to side. "Nothing but clothes in here. Nothing." He pulled his head out and closed the door.

"Thanks," Payton whispered and rolled onto his side.

"On or off? The light?" his dad asked again.

"On, please."

"Okay. Call me if you need anything. I'll leave the door open and I'll be just in the kitchen, all right?"

"Okay."

With one last tender look, his father left the room then poked his head back inside the door. "I love you, Payton."

"I love you, too."

His father left.

Payton closed his eyes. Images of the dead danced before his mind's eye.

He coughed, swallowed, then coughed again.

His eyes shot open as the taste of rotten fish filled his mouth.

Black smoke trickled out the corners of his lips.

ABOUT THE AUTHOR

A.P. Fuchs is the author of many novels and short stories, most of which have been published. He is also known for his superhero series, *The Axiom-man Saga*, and is the author of *Blood of the Dead*, the first novel in the shoot 'em up zombie trilogy, *Undead World*.

Fuchs lives and writes in Winnipeg, Manitoba, with his wife, Roxanne, and two sons, Gabriel and Lewis.

Visit his corner of the Web at
www.apfuchs.com

Check out the *Undead World Trilogy* at
www.undeadworldtrilogy.com

FLIGHT. STRENGTH. ENERGY BEAMS. POWER.

THE Axiom-man™ SAGA

One night Gabriel Garrison was visited by a nameless messenger who bestowed upon him great power, a power intended for good. Once discovering what this power was and what it enabled him to do, Gabriel became Axiom-man, a symbol of hope in a city that had none.

Ask for the series at your local bookstore.

Also available at your favorite on-line retailer

1-897217-57-9

978-1-897217-71-9

978-1-897217-69-6

978-1-897217-83-2

WWW.AXIOM-MAN.COM

COSCOM ENTERTAINMENT

Where Imagination is Truth

www.coscomentertainment.com